Ryder took a step toward Faith to really look into her eyes.

"You're pregnant?" he asked, knowing full well that he'd be able to tell if she faltered. She'd never been able to meet his eyes and flat-out lie. Or at least that's what he'd believed. How much did he really get to know her in the few months they'd spent together? She'd already shocked him once by walking out. And now she'd thrown him the last news he'd expected to hear from her.

"Yes," she said, plain as day.

"And the child is mine?"

"Yes," she said with that same certainty.

She wasn't lying.

"If that's true—and I need a little time to process that fact—why are you telling me now?"

"Like I said, I need your help and I'll do whatever it takes to get it," she said, her gaze a study in determination.

"You know this qualifies as blackmail."

"Does that mean you'll help me?" The first spark of hope lit her face.

TEXAS-SIZED TROUBLE

USA TODAY Bestselling Author

BARB HAN

Many thanks to Allison Lyons and Jill Marsal, the best editor and agent I could hope to have the privilege with which to work.

Brandon and Tori, the two of you make everyday life a joyful adventure. I love you both!

Babe, you are forever the love of my life. Can you believe one of our babies turns eighteen this month?

Jacob, aka Jakey Bear, February used to be a cold, short month until you were born, filling our world with sunshine and warmth. Eighteen years have gone by in a flash, and our journey has been a lot like Texas weather: exciting, full of sunshine and *always* an adventure! College is close, a job will follow, and no matter how far away you venture, home will always be your soft place to land. We love you!

ISBN-13: 978-0-373-75657-5

Texas-Sized Trouble

PLEASE RECYCLE • THIS PRODUCT IS RECYCLABLE •

Recycling programs for this product may not exist in your area.

This edition published by arrangement with Harlequin Books S.A.

For questions and comments about the quality of this book, please contact us at CustomerService@Harlequin.com.

HARLEQUIN®
www.Harlequin.com

Printed in U.S.A.

USA TODAY bestselling author **Barb Han** lives in north Texas with her very own hero-worthy husband, three beautiful children, a spunky golden retriever/standard poodle mix and too many books in her to-read pile. In her downtime, she plays video games and spends much of her time on or around a basketball court. She loves interacting with readers and is grateful for their support. You can reach her at barbhan.com.

Books by Barb Han

Harlequin Intrigue

Cattlemen Crime Club

Stockyard Snatching
Delivering Justice
One Tough Texan
Texas-Sized Trouble

Mason Ridge

Texas Prey
Texas Takedown
Texas Hunt
Texan's Baby

The Campbells of Creek Bend

Witness Protection
Gut Instinct
Hard Target

Rancher Rescue

Harlequin Intrigue Noir

Atomic Beauty

CAST OF CHARACTERS

Faith McCabe—A forbidden romance leads to pregnancy, and there's no way her family would ever accept an O'Brien child. When her half brother turns up missing, she has nowhere to turn but to the man she walked away from, who happens to be her baby's father. Can she deny her heart in order to protect the man and unborn child she loves?

Ryder O'Brien—This elder twin likes life on the edge. He's competitive and enjoys having a good time, but after tragically losing his parents, he found more than comfort in a forbidden romance. He'll set aside his anger to help the woman he can't seem to forget, but can he risk his heart one more time?

Nicholas Bowden—The half brother Faith is risking her life to find.

Hollister McCabe—How much does he really know about the kidnapping?

Karen McCabe—This wife has endured far too much living with Hollister McCabe. Has she finally snapped?

Celeste Bowden—Nicholas's mother doesn't have warm feelings for Hollister McCabe. He got her pregnant fifteen years ago and turned his back on her and the baby. Would she go to any lengths to blackmail him?

The Hattie brothers—Are they behind the kidnapping or just pawns in a twisted game?

Hannah—Is she the mastermind behind the kidnapping or an innocent victim?

Tommy Johnson—The sheriff who grew up at the O'Brien ranch and considers them family.

Chapter One

There was a chill in the air, the promise of a cold front moving in on the last day of winter. Texas weather in early March was unpredictable. Ryder O'Brien walked toward his pickup and saw Faith McCabe leaning against his ride. He didn't do regret. So why, all of a sudden, was he filled with it as he walked toward her? Those long legs tucked into tan fringed ankle boots. Her white off-the-shoulder dress contrasted against the long chestnut waves cascading over her shoulders, and ended slightly above midthigh. He didn't want to notice those details about her. Ending their affair and walking away from her hadn't exactly been a choice. She'd burned him. Thinking about how easy it had been for her to break off their relationship made him frown and stirred residual anger.

"What are you doing here?" he ground out.

"I came to see you," she said, folding her arms like when she was secretly insecure but needed to cover.

"We have nothing to talk about." He clenched his teeth. He could acknowledge to himself that his words were angry. It had been only a few months since their affair ended. His feelings were still raw. She looked good, though, and that frustrated the hell out of him.

"I do," she hedged, flashing her eyes at him.

"What's wrong? None of your other boyfriends around?" Ryder stopped. There was no need to get close enough to see the gold flecks in her honey browns. "You're wasting your time."

"I need a favor." Her right shoulder dipped, another move that gave away her true insecurity at being there. She might be trying to stand tall and come off as confident, but Ryder could still read her despite the show she was putting on.

"Then you're wasting *my* time," he said. The last thing he needed was to trust that she was different from her family. He'd taken that bait once and been burned. "Let me save us both the energy. The answer is no."

Her cool facade broke. "Please, I'm desp—"

"It's a little late to play the innocent 'help

me' card, don't you think?" he shot back, anger replacing any trace of regret. He looked her up and down, not holding back the annoyance in his glare. "You broke off our…whatever we were doing…with a Post-it note. Who even uses those anymore?"

Yeah, he was letting his anger get the best of him. He couldn't help it. His pride had taken a huge hit. When it came to Faith and the way she'd left things, he couldn't keep cool.

"I'm sorry about the method, but I only said what we both knew. Anything more than good sex between us would be asking too much," she said, and he knew she believed that. To say their families had deep-seated bad blood running between them was a lot like saying werewolves turned at a full moon.

"Whatever," he said as dismissively as he could, given the fact that his pulse pounded and his body seemed keenly aware of hers. Another detail he didn't want to overthink.

"I wouldn't be here if it wasn't important, Ryder." The sound of his name on her tongue made him feel things he didn't want to. But then everything about Faith stirred up unwanted emotions inside him. She might've been right about them not having a future, but they would never know now, not after the way she'd handled things. He could admit to being curious about what she thought he could help her with, though. *Hold on.* That was exactly the thinking that had gotten him in trouble in the first place.

Faith McCabe had always been off-limits to Ryder, and that was most likely the reason he couldn't resist sneaking around to spend time with her a few months ago and not because of a real connection. He'd always been a renegade at heart, always bucking the system and insisting on handling his life his own way. But when his and Faith's relationship had started getting serious and, in his view, interesting, she'd retreated and refused to see or speak to him again. He chalked his current feelings of betrayal up to a bruised ego.

When he'd stepped into the parking lot of the Dusty Trail Bar and Grill and saw her standing there, it was more than muscle memory that had him on edgc. Faith still looked good, too good. Her skin was glowing and her hair shone under the lamplight. He couldn't help but go to that place in his head—the one where she lay in his arms until morning after a long night of making love. And that was about as productive as washing down a jalapeño with gasoline.

"What is it? You miss me?" he asked, trying to goad her into the fight they should've had months ago. Not being able to say his piece was probably the reason he'd held on to the hurt this long.

The pinched look she shot him next said she didn't appreciate the sarcasm.

Her gaze shifted until she was studying the toe of her boot a little too intently. Even now, he couldn't deny a draw toward Faith, or a need to protect her. But then instincts were as hardwired as attraction.

"I have a half brother who's gone missing," she started without looking up, a sign that her confidence had waned.

"And you're telling me this because?" Ryder asked, not giving an inch, maintaining the intensity of his glare. This was news to him, although with a father like Hollister McCabe anything was possible. The man and Ryder's father couldn't have been more opposite, and that was part of the reason they'd clashed when his father was alive. Ryder suppressed a sarcastic laugh. *Clashed* put their conflict lightly. When McCabe had tried to strong-arm Ryder's father for a piece of the family land years ago, they'd almost gone toe-to-toe and had been bitter enemies ever since.

"He's in danger, Ryder. I know he is. He lives two towns over with a mother who hustles drinks at a dive bar and leaves him alone days on end to fend for himself." She started to walk toward Ryder and then stopped, glancing up pensively.

He didn't need her moving any closer. Not with the way his pulse pounded already, reminding him of the strength of the attraction he'd once held. So much had changed in the past couple of months, including him. The sobering reality that came with learning his parents had been murdered had made Ryder a different man. After hearing the news, he'd taken leave from the successful transportation company he'd started and returned home to Bluff, Texas. Running tourists back and forth from the airport to various ski resorts in the Denver area was a big change from his life in Texas, and he was ready to take his rightful place alongside his brothers running the family cattle ranch and rifleman's club, nicknamed the Cattlemen Crime Club. The best perk of running his company had been that he'd spent many days pushing his own limits on the mountain. Coming home had been the right thing to do but didn't offer the adrenaline rushes he craved. Dating Faith on the side had most likely been an attempt to reclaim some of his renegade ways and blow off steam, he tried to convince himself again. The thought of real feelings developing between an O'Brien and a McCabe had the word *avalanche* written all over it. That's exactly what it would be—out of control and devastating to everything it touched.

Hence, the thrill, a little voice in his head reminded.

"Sounds like a bad situation all around," he said, not wanting to let anything she had to say twist his emotions. Faith had a way of getting under his skin, and he had no intention of giving her permission to use him again. "Call child welfare and report her."

"They'll just take him away, throw him in the system, and I'll lose track of him. At least now I can watch over him." She took a tentative step forward and then rubbed her arms like she was trying to stave off the chill. She needed a coat, but it wasn't Ryder's place to tell her.

"Whoa. Not so fast." He held up his hands to stop her from coming any closer in case she decided to play on his weakness for her again. It wouldn't work. Burn him once, shame on her. Burn him twice, and he deserved everything he got. Ryder knew better than to touch a hot stove twice, and he'd been taught both sayings as a kid. He'd be damned if she threw flames his way a second time. "Tell me why this concerns me, Faith."

"It doesn't. Not directly." She straightened her back and folded her arms across her chest. "He's a good kid, well, teenager, and he doesn't deserve the life he was given."

"Why come to me? Why not ask Trouble for help?" It was a low blow bringing up one of her exes, and Ryder felt the same sensation as a physical punch at thinking about her together with Trouble. Again, Ryder reminded himself that Faith couldn't be trusted. She'd proved that to him and everyone else in town when she'd shown up with Timmy "Trouble" Hague a week after cutting ties with Ryder and claiming the two were in a relationship. There was nothing worse to Ryder than having his nose rubbed in a breakup. She didn't stop with Trouble. She'd dated several others like him within a monthlong span. She hadn't needed to convince Ryder to walk away by parading a new man in front of him every week. The Post-it had done the trick.

"Hear me out, please," she pleaded, and he was having a difficult time ignoring the fact that her teeth were chattering. He didn't want to care.

"Step aside. I have plans tonight," Ryder said, unmoved. Or, at least that was the vibe he was trying to give off. Internally, he was at war. Those residual feelings had a stronghold and he couldn't afford to let them dig their heels in further, because they were tempting him to give in and agree to help her. He tried to convince himself that being a Texan would make him hardwired to help any woman in trouble and that the pull had nothing to do with the fact that it was Faith.

"Can we go somewhere we can talk?" she asked, her gaze darting around. Was she afraid to be seen with him?

Seriously? After running around with Trouble?

"Like your bedroom?" Ryder scoffed. "Sorry, sweet cheeks. That ship has sailed."

Her hurt look made him almost wish he hadn't said that. As far as he was concerned, she didn't have the right to look pained. It wasn't her heart that had been stomped all over.

Even so, guilt nipped at him for the low blow, and he half expected her to give up and walk away. He was making sticking around as hard on her as he could without being a complete jerk.

She didn't budge. She just stood there shivering.

"Spit it out. What do you want from me?"

he demanded, not wanting to drag this conversation out more than necessary. He was tired and this was taking a toll. He had plans with a soft pillow. It was late, and work on the ranch started at 5:00 a.m. sharp.

"I need your help finding Nicholas." Her eyes pleaded.

"You need a coat," Ryder said.

"What?" She seemed surprised.

"You look cold." Ryder motioned toward her arms.

"Mine's in the car," she said. "And I'll get it as soon as you agree to help."

"Can't you microchip kids these days? Or, better yet, why not just call him and wait for him to get back to you like a normal person?" He put his hand up between them. "Oh, wait, I forgot. You're not a normal person. I should've known a McCabe wouldn't have time for common sense or following the rules."

Faith sucked in a burst of air. That comment scored a direct hit. Ryder should feel a sense of satisfaction. He didn't.

"He's somewhere hurt or he's been taken and I'm worried," she said, recovering. Her gaze locked onto his.

"Take out an ad or check his social media pages. Kids love to broadcast their locations for the world to see." Besides, Ryder had other, more pressing things to focus on, like bringing justice to the person who'd murdered his parents.

"He's not that kind of kid and I already checked—" her tone rose in panic before she seemed able to recover and reel it in "—or I wouldn't be here." She had that no-other-choice quality to her tone. Again, Ryder had to ask himself why she thought it was a good idea to come to him. He didn't figure she'd give an honest response. So, she was genuinely concerned about her half brother. Good for her. Maybe it proved she had half a heart in that chest of hers after all. That was about as far as Ryder was willing to go.

"I'm sorry about your family being messed up, but being in the perfect one isn't as easy as it looks. Everyone's got problems," Ryder snapped, needing to keep emotional distance between them. In truth, he loved his brothers. They were a close-knit bunch and about as perfect as a genuine family could be. Sure, they had issues from time to time, but they always managed to work out their differences. He and his twin brother, Joshua, were especially close. "And I'm done here."

"I have to find him and I'm not giving up. It will put me in danger if I go alone but I don't have a choice, Ryder. I have to do it," she said, standing her ground yet again. The sound of his name rolling off her tongue had always stirred his chest in a way he couldn't afford to allow. This time was no different. All his warning bells sounded.

"Sounds like you're making a big mistake." He shrugged. "Free country."

"Do you really hate me that much?" she asked, and the desperation in her tone struck a chord. "You'd allow an innocent kid to be hurt just to prove a point?"

Now it was his turn to take in a sharp breath.

"No. But I can't help you, either." Maybe he could take a second to talk her out of being stupid. "If you're really worried about this kid, call Tommy. The sheriff would be better at tracking down a missing teenager than me. Besides, you know the reality as much as I do. The kid's most likely having fun with his friends. He'll check in once he sobers up in a couple of days."

"Tommy is friends with your family, not mine. He won't help a McCabe and you know it," she said defensively.

The chilly air goose-bumped her arms and Ryder had to stop himself from offering his jacket. Chivalry was ingrained in him, and he had to fight against his own cowboy code so that she wouldn't think she was getting to him. Give her an inch and she'd stomp on him again with those fringed boots.

"Even so, he's the law and he'll help you," Ryder said. "He took an oath, and he takes it seriously."

"Braxton is a few counties over and out of his jurisdiction. That's where Nicholas lives," she said.

"Tommy can make a few calls, do a little digging. If it makes you feel better, I'll ask him myself." Ryder had no clue why he'd just volunteered himself like that. He'd have time to curse himself later. The sheriff in Braxton wasn't exactly known for being cooperative.

An anguished sound tore from her throat. "That's not good enough, and Tommy doesn't care about Nicholas. I need answers now and I'm afraid something very bad has happened to him. I can't afford to lose any more time, and someone follows me when I check on him."

Didn't that get all of Ryder's neck hairs to stand on end?

"What makes you think so?" he asked.

"I drove to Nicholas's house to check on him when he stopped responding to my texts three days ago and an SUV followed me to the county line."

"Could've been random," he said.

"I've been out there every night, and last night the SUV tapped my bumper," she said, rubbing her arms as if the memory gave her chills instead of the cold night air.

Ryder didn't like that. He'd take a minute to consider her position. He could concede that she'd had a point a few seconds ago. Tommy wasn't likely to go above and beyond the call of duty for a McCabe. He'd arrested her brothers, who were immediately bailed out by the family lawyer too many times to have sympathy for any of them, even Faith.

Her concern for her half brother seemed genuine. Ryder could tell based on the desperation in her honey browns. If the situation were reversed and one of his brothers had gone missing, he'd do whatever it took to find him. All five of his siblings were grown now, and good men, but they'd gotten themselves into a few tricky situations as teenagers. Ryder could buy the idea that a good kid could get into trouble. He had a harder time swallowing the idea that a McCabe offspring could be anything but trouble. Bad was in their blood. He'd believed Faith to be different from her family, and look how that had worked out for him.

"How do you know he's missing exactly?" he asked.

"We talk every day without fail. I was supposed to help him with geometry homework and he stood me up. He's never done that. Ever." Her wide eyes conveyed panic and worry. When he examined her features, he saw how tired and worried she looked.

"Have you spoken to his mother?" The teenager could have gotten himself in over his head or involved in drugs. Even so, none of this concerned Ryder, and Faith hadn't given him one solid reason he should get involved. With her family's money, she could hire an investigator.

"We're not exactly on good terms and I have nothing to say to the woman," Faith said, and her left shoulder shot up. He'd seen that move before. She was being indignant.

From his viewpoint, a quick phone call could most likely clear this whole thing up. If Faith was too stubborn to make that call she didn't need to be reaching out to him to do her dirty work.

"Then I can't help you. That was my only card. I'm folding. If you really believe he's missing, then you should talk to someone in law enforcement. His mother might've reported his disappearance already." He threw his hands up in surrender. As it was, he was having a difficult time keeping a wall between them and maintaining his neutral position. A woman in trouble wasn't something he could normally turn his back on. He blamed his Texas upbringing and the fact that he'd had amazing parents.

"I'll sweeten the pot," she said quickly.

"You don't have anything I want," Ryder said, pushing thoughts of how soft her skin had been when he ran his finger along the curves of her stomach out of his mind. Or how much the sound of her laughter had temporarily suspended the pain of losing his parents.

"You want to know the real reason I walked away from you, Ryder O'Brien?" Now she was the one who was angry. He could see the fire in her eyes. Good. She'd get mad, spit out a few hostile words meant to offend him and then leave.

Problem solved.

"It doesn't matter." But his wounded pride said something else entirely—he wanted to know.

"You sure about that?" she asked in her one-last-chance tone.

"Have never been more certain of anything in my life." If she wanted his help, making him angry was the wrong way to go about it.

He didn't like the idea of her putting herself in danger if that was the case, and he'd tried reasoning with her by telling her to bring in the law. If she didn't have enough sense to stay out of harm's way there wasn't much he could do about it. "Why ask me to help in the first place? You had to know that I would refuse. You're not exactly high on my list of people I want to see again."

"You won't turn me down. I know you and there's something I've been keeping from you…" She paused long enough to put her hands on her belly. "Anything happens to me and your child goes with me. You're going to be a father, Ryder. And that's why I left you. If anyone found out this was your child, then my life, heck, *your life*, would be over."

"Good one, Faith." She wasn't afraid to pull out all the stops on…

Hold on a damn minute. The look on her face slapped him with a new reality. Was she serious?

"That's right, Ryder. I'm carrying your child." Her lip quivered even though her words rolled off her tongue steady as steel.

She wasn't lying?

He stood there for a long moment and stared at her, daring her to break the glaring contest and tell him she was joking. There was no way…

Was there?

A memory came back to him in a rush. He remembered one time when they'd been so lost and so into each other during their love-making neither had noticed that the condom he wore broke.

Okay, so it was *possible.* But that didn't mean…

Ryder took a step toward Faith to really look into her eyes.

"You're pregnant?" he asked, knowing full well that he'd be able to tell if she faltered. She'd never been able to look him in the eyes and flat-out lie. Or at least that's what he'd believed. How much did he get to know the real her in the few months they'd spent time together? She'd already shocked him once by walking out. And now she'd thrown him the last news he'd expected to hear from her.

"Yes," she said plain as day.

"And the child is mine?"

"Yes," she said with that same certainty.

She wasn't lying.

"If that's true—and I need a little time to come to terms with that fact—why are you telling me now?" he asked, trying to absorb that news. He couldn't begin to process the idea of becoming a father, and he wasn't immediately sure how he felt about it. All he knew was that his life was about to change forever. He'd seen firsthand the effects of the baby boom on the ranch with a few of his brothers.

"Like I said, I need your help and I'll do whatever it takes to get it," she said, her gaze a study in determination.

"Including lie about me fathering your child?" He'd thrown that question out to see if he could knock her off balance.

She stood her ground. "We both know I'm not."

"Then I expect you to take care of yourself. Running straight into a fire doesn't exactly fit that bill," he said, and he meant every word. Until they sorted this mess out and knew for sure that she was, in fact, pregnant and he was the father of her child, he expected her to treat herself like a princess.

A thought struck. Was there any chance she could be so desperate for help that she'd bluff to get him to agree to help her?

Ryder studied her expression. If she was lying, she was a pro. Then again, he hadn't seen their breakup coming, either. He'd need time to digest the possibility of being a father, especially considering all that he'd been through in the past few months. He forced his thoughts away from the fact that she'd been his sole comfort during the most difficult time of his life and their relationship had been about more than just the sex. It was saying a lot that they could be so into each other that a condom had broken and neither one realized until it was too late. Sex with Faith had been right up there with the best of his life. If he was being honest, it topped the list. Not something he cared to admit right now or dwell on too much. Even though the sex was great, there'd been so much more. He wasn't normally one for a lot of words but holding her in their afterglow and doing just that—talking—had been even better than the sex. And that was saying a helluva lot.

"You know this qualifies as blackmail," he said, his brain refusing to fully comprehend the news. He'd want a DNA test to be sure. And if the results proved his paternity, then he'd do what a man should—take care of his own.

"Does that mean you'll help me?"

"GET IN. YOU'RE DAMN right we need to talk. Not here where everyone can see us," Ryder said, opening the passenger door of his pickup and then walking around to the driver's side without waiting for her to climb inside.

Faith almost backed out after seeing the hurt in his eyes after dropping the pregnancy bomb. She thought better of it. Yes, he was angry at her, but she'd realized that it was the only way to secure his help, and he was the only person she could trust right now.

All plans to find the perfect time to tell him about the pregnancy and have a civil conversation had flown out the window with her desperation. What she'd said was true, though. Her life would be over if her father found out she was carrying an O'Brien child.

"Don't take me home or into town," Faith said as she positioned herself in the seat of his dual-cab pickup and then buckled in. She hadn't expected to play the pregnancy card with Ryder, but she was frantic. His shocked reaction braided her stomach lining.

Seeing him again had hurt like hell and she was still trying to regain her balance. He looked even better than she remembered with those sharp jet-black eyes and dark hair. He was six feet three inches of masculine muscle. And even angry, he was gorgeous. Walking away from him after finding out she was pregnant had nearly killed her, but she'd been his temporary shelter in a storm—a storm that was about to become a hurricane. Once the storm blew over and he regained his bearings he would've realized the same thing she had—a McCabe and an O'Brien didn't stand a chance.

"What? Afraid to be seen with me?" he bit out. His voice poured over her, netting a physical reaction she couldn't afford.

"Of course not." She did her best to shake off his bitter tone. It was a temporary reaction to having his world rocked. He needed a minute to cool off so he could start thinking rationally again. It was a good sign that he wanted to talk. Deep down, he was a good man.

Besides, Faith could relate to the emotions that had to be zipping through him right now. The pregnancy wasn't supposed to happen. The decisions she'd made after weren't supposed to be part of her plans. And all that was predicated on the fact that she wasn't supposed to fall for an O'Brien, let alone the renegade twin brother. And that was probably it. Her attraction was so strong because he was exciting and a breath of fresh air. Ryder had always been so alive, when she'd felt restricted for so many years living under her parents' roof with three older brothers watching her every move. The family's double standard that the boys could run buck wild and she had to practically be a nun had been suffocating.

Ryder represented danger and excitement, and her foolish heart had fallen hard for him when she'd seen him wandering around the lake, looking lost after news of his parents had made headlines. Everything about the O'Briens was news. Murder had been beyond scandal.

The next few months of their relationship had been insane and incredible. Secret rendezvous at his fishing cabin. Both of them escaping reality and getting lost in each other. Talking for hours into the night. She'd almost forgotten that he was an O'Brien and she was a McCabe until she'd overheard him on his cell phone with his brother, cursing her father, questioning whether he'd had anything to do with his parents' murders.

She could understand his distrust of her father. The man was a shrewd businessman and even she could admit that he pushed the legal boundaries beyond their limits. Worse to her, the man was a philanderer, and she'd watched her mother fade over the years as she accepted his behavior even though he could be quite charming when he wanted to be. But murder?

Her father might have loose morals and no

conscience when it came to business, but he wasn't capable of killing anyone.

And then another blow had come when Ryder's brother asked where Ryder was and what he was doing all those times he'd been with her. He'd responded that he hadn't been doing anything special. He'd just been getting away for fresh air and spending time alone to sort out his thoughts.

Reality had been a hard slap. Spending time with her hadn't been as special to him as it had been to her. They'd been sneaking around like teenagers and she started to wonder if the reason was because he'd been embarrassed to be seen with her. He would always be an O'Brien and she would always be a McCabe. And he, like everyone in Bluff, would always see her in a different light because of it.

When she'd learned that she was pregnant, she panicked. A real life with Ryder was out of the question. Dating Trouble and the others had been her way of throwing everyone off the trail, including Ryder. He wouldn't want a McCabe baby any more than her parents would ever accept an O'Brien. It would be bad enough in her parents' eyes that she was pregnant without being married, but having an O'Brien in the family would be all-out war. Not only would her parents make her life miserable but they'd make her unborn child miserable, too.

And that wasn't even the worst of it. She feared that Ryder—who was just spending time with her, not getting serious—would want to man up and do the right thing by his child. His Texas upbringing would influence him, and he'd probably propose marriage. If hormones got the best of her—and they had made her crazy so far—she might actually accept. And then what?

Would they stay together for the sake of the child eighteen unhappy years until said kid went off to college and the two of them could finally separate? That's exactly what her parents had done. Her own mother had been forced to come back and had never been the same. Faith's father didn't curb his appetite for chasing pretty much anything in a skirt. Faith had known since she was old enough to figure out what was happening. And her mother was broken. Still broken. She seemed different lately. Worse, if that was even possible.

Faith's siblings seemed blind to it all. And they were another reason a relationship between her and Ryder could never work...if her father didn't kill him, her brothers would. The O'Briens and McCabes were worse than oil and water. They were gasoline and forest fire.

Even so, maybe it was good that her secret was out. Working side by side, she could convince Ryder the best course of action would be to keep the secret. Surely he would come to the same conclusion she had. Besides, she had a plan.

Break the news and each guy she'd gone out with would distance himself from any suspicion of being the father of her child. And then she could tell her parents that she wanted to bring up her baby alone. She didn't really care who the father was, even though her heart screamed at her that she did. Her father wouldn't interfere with her plans to leave town. Heck, he'd tell her to get out after embarrassing him. And then she and her baby could live in peace. That was the only real chance her child had of growing up normal.

Righteous or not, telling Ryder complicated her plans. Had she really believed that she could've left town without telling him about the baby? She'd initially feared that he'd put two and two together when news of her pregnancy broke. And that's exactly the reason she'd handled their breakup the way she had. The O'Briens were proud, honest men. And her actions had been the only way to ensure Ryder wouldn't do anything stupid, like propose marriage for the baby's sake and ruin both their lives. A fist tightened in her stomach. *Breathe.*

She'd take things one step at a time. For now, she'd secure Ryder's help. Finding Nicholas had to be her top priority even if it meant turning her life upside down.

"Getting out anytime soon or do you plan to sit in here all night?" Ryder asked, and he sounded concerned.

Faith hadn't realized the pickup had stopped. "Yeah, sure." She blinked at him.

He sat there, staring at her, making everything harder than she expected. In her heart of hearts she'd known that she couldn't keep the pregnancy secret from him forever. Her obstetrician had said she could expect to start showing soon. This being the first pregnancy had bought her some extra time and she could easily cover what was going on so far.

Time was supposed to bring wisdom as to how she should handle sharing the news. It hadn't. She hadn't breathed a word to anyone. And keeping a secret like this had been more than difficult. It felt good to finally tell someone about the baby, but she needed to stay on track. None of her problems seemed as important or immediate as finding Nicholas.

The sky was pitch-black as she climbed out of the truck. The chilly air nipped at her through her dress. She wished she'd worn a coat as she shivered. Normally, the hot hormones had her wishing she could pack herself in ice. Not today.

A blanket of clouds covered the stars. It was too dark outside to see where he'd taken her, and she'd been in a daze for the ride over, not paying attention. As she gained her footing in the gravel it hit her. Ryder had taken her to the fishing cabin.

A wall of memories crashed around her. This was the place they'd met countless times, made love more than she cared to remember… and she'd lost her heart.

Doubts crept in as to whether or not she was doing the right thing being with Ryder at all with every step toward the cabin. He had the power to crush her with a few words.

"Maybe we should go somewhere else to talk." Panic squeezed her chest as she approached the basic log cabin. A reasonable voice overrode her emotions. Ryder was the only one she could tell about Nicholas and the only one who understood how much was at stake as she made the decision to locate him.

"No one will find us here. Isn't that what you want?" His deep voice, warm and soothing, was like pouring whiskey over crackling ice.

"Yes," she conceded, very aware of the masculine presence behind her, guiding her with his hand on the small of her back.

Chapter Two

Faith sat on the edge of the couch in the living room, ignoring the sensual shivers climbing up her arms. She wished she could block out memories as easily. The last time she and Ryder had been at the cabin, their naked bodies had been entwined until morning.

Tall, with the muscles of a well-honed athlete, Ryder had a physical appeal that hadn't dimmed in the least and her hormones had all of her senses heightened. His dark hair framed a squared jaw, and he had the most piercing jet-black eyes. Everything about the way he looked communicated strength, confidence and a little bit of danger. And after the news she'd broken, fierceness. All of which would be a good thing if she could harness it toward helping find Nicholas.

"Take me back to the beginning. How do

you know the baby is mine?" Ryder's question was a bullet to the heart.

"You were the only option," she fired back, and her plan of using the other men to throw everyone off the trail seemed to dawn on him.

"Did you plan on telling me eventually?" he asked after another uneasy minute had passed.

"Yes, and we can discuss anything else you want after we find Nicholas." She needed to direct the conversation back on task.

"Holding a pregnancy over my head is blackmail, Faith." His normally strong, all-male persona faded with the look of confusion in his dark eyes.

She hated that this was her fault. Well, not the pregnancy. It'd taken two to dance that tango. She took the blame for the way Ryder was finding out. Seeing the hurt in his eyes knifed her. But she needed to stay strong for Nicholas's sake and not let anything else derail her from her search. She knew in her heart that her brother was in trouble. "I'm sorry for how this has gone down, Ryder. I truly am. But I'm desperate to find Nicholas and you weren't going to help me any other way."

He seemed to take a minute to contemplate that thought while he assessed her, his attention on her belly.

"How much longer before the baby comes?" he asked.

"I'm almost five months along," she said, her hand instinctively coming up to her stomach.

"Boy or girl?" His voice was steel, giving nothing away of his emotions now.

"One of those," she said. Having her doctor tell her the sex of the baby made it that much more real. For that reason, she'd decided to wait. And then there was the fact that it seemed wrong to know without the father present.

"They don't know?"

"I asked my doctor not to tell me," she said.

Another few minutes of silence passed. Her need to press Ryder in order to get his agreement to help find Nicholas warred with her better judgment. She'd played her hand with Ryder and there wasn't much more she could do to follow the trail without his help, not without the possibility of putting their baby at risk given that the SUV driver was becoming more aggressive.

Three days was a long time to be missing. Anything could be happening to her little brother right now…

Tears burst through just thinking about any harm coming to Nicholas.

"I'm sorry," she said, trying to pull it together, "it's just hormones giving me mood swings. They make it hard to think rationally."

Ryder studied her.

"How do you know your half brother didn't get fed up with his mother and run away?" he asked as she tried to force her gaze away from his lips—lips that made her body zing with awareness at the thought of how he'd once used the tip of his tongue to trail her curves. Faith admonished herself. That thought couldn't be more inappropriate under the circumstances. Her hormones didn't just make her emotional. They made her miss having sex even more.

"We had plans, and besides, he would've told me," she said.

"You sure about that? Even people you think you know can shock the hell out of you." Ryder's tense, aggressive posture would strike fear in any reasonable person. She knew him well enough to know that he would never do anything to hurt her.

Faith told herself nothing mattered more than getting his agreement to help find Nicholas. And she was making gains on that front; she could tell by how bunched his face muscles looked and the tic over his left eye—all positive signs she was making headway. He was in conflict with himself and that was a good thing for her. The very fact that he'd agreed to discuss the matter privately was her first real step in the right direction. She could put up with his intense scrutiny if it meant gaining his agreement to find her brother.

"As sure as I can be. We're close. I've been checking on him ever since I found out about him, so around kindergarten, and he doesn't have any other siblings. Well, none that he knows," she said. "My brothers would never acknowledge him if they knew, and he's so much better than they are anyway. I would do anything I could to keep them separate and make sure they had no influence over him."

This wasn't the time to recount all the shortcomings of McCabe men.

"Why do you know about him but your brothers don't?" he asked. It was a fair question.

"I spent summers working for my dad. I was being groomed for the family business and my job was learning the paperwork. I don't have to tell you how much running a ranch is about dealing with stacks of documents. Legal papers were on my dad's desk. I guess they got mixed up with a stack of bills. He was being sued for child support by Nicholas's mother. You can imagine how that turned out. My dad got himself out of paying. Actually his lawyers did. So I've been sneaking money to Nicholas for the past ten years."

"How do you know he's your blood relative?" he asked.

She retrieved her cell phone from her purse and then scrolled through pictures, stopping at a recent one of her and Nicholas together. She held out her phone to Ryder so he could see.

"There's no denying the resemblance," he said, studying the likeness.

"He looks like a mini, younger version of Jason, only he's nicer." Jason was the youngest of her three brothers and her senior by four years. He'd been the toughest, too, having spent his life proving to his two older brothers, Jesse and Jimmy, that he could hold his own.

"I've learned not to trust the actions of any McCabe," Ryder said flatly. He was obviously referring to her walking out and the pregnancy news.

She had that coming.

Glancing down at her stomach, she said, "I didn't do this alone."

Ryder made a face like he was about to say something hateful and seemed to think better of it, when he pressed his lips into a thin line instead.

"It's probably for the best if we stick to the reason we're here. *For now,*" Ryder said. Those last two words came out as a warning she knew better than to disregard.

"Fine." She had no doubt the two of them would be doing a lot of talking about the future of their baby once the dust settled. A very large part of her had been dreading the inevitable conversation with him for months now and yet another side couldn't deny that she wanted to involve Ryder. The first trimester had been too much about trying to keep food down to worry about what she would say to him. Who knew morning sickness actually meant throwing up all day? Her queasiness had finally let up a couple of weeks ago and she'd been trying to plan out her words ever since. She'd tried to convince herself that it would be a good idea to leave town without ever telling Ryder. She knew in her heart that she could never do that to him. No matter how strong the arguments against it waged inside her head, he had a right to know.

Ryder pulled a chair from the kitchenette, turned it around backward and straddled it opposite the coffee table. "Tell me what really has you so worried."

"Nicholas might be a McCabe but he's nothing like the boys in my family, despite having a worthless mother. He's fifteen and plays on the school soccer team. His grades are good. He's always talking about a future, getting a scholarship, going to college," she said, probably more defensively than she'd intended. "He's a decent kid, Ryder."

"If that were completely true, we wouldn't be having this conversation." Ryder had a way of looking right through her. She worried he'd see her fear while she was trying to put up a brave front.

"That's why none of this makes sense. He wouldn't just disappear like that. He's not that kind of kid."

Ryder's look of disbelief struck a bad chord.

"I know you can't stand my family and you may never trust me again, but I know Nicholas wouldn't up and disappear without telling me," she said, hating the defensiveness in her tone. Ryder's not believing her hurt more than it should.

"What else do you know about his life besides what I could read on a college application? Have you met any of his friends?" Ryder asked.

"We kept our relationship secret. So, no," she said honestly.

"Seems you're full of deceptions," he shot

back. "I'm guessing that's why I never heard about him before."

Her first instinct was to fight back. She let that zinger go for the sake of her little brother, even though it scored a direct hit. Common sense said that arguing with Ryder wouldn't get her what she needed. Besides, a little piece of her knew that Ryder had every right to be upset with her and he was still reacting to the bomb she'd dropped on him. She should've gone to him with the news or given him a better reason for the breakup, instead of chickening out while she was waiting for him so they could talk and deciding to scribble her exit on the only thing she had in her purse, a Post-it.

"My father went to great lengths to cover up his relationship with Nicholas's mother. I thought he might dish out repercussions against the two of them if he knew I was seeing my brother. That's the reason for the deception. I couldn't risk telling anyone. Not even you," she said.

"He would've been angry with you, too. Are you sure you weren't protecting yourself?" Ryder said in that unnerving steady tone.

"I don't care what happens to me," she retorted. "Or at least I didn't until now." She touched her belly.

"What about your mom?"

"I was fairly sure she had no idea about Nicholas. But she's been acting stranger than usual lately. Jumpy. But that could just be a change in her anxiety medication."

"Self-preservation seems to be a genetic survival trait in McCabe women," he said in a low enough voice that she could still hear it.

She chose not to respond.

"What are you really afraid Nicholas got himself into?" Ryder asked.

She shot him a grateful look for the change in subject. "He wouldn't stand me up without a good reason, and he always responds to my texts. I'm afraid for him, Ryder."

"Could he have a recreational drinking or drug habit?"

"No." Her shoulders slumped forward. "He has a good head on his shoulders. He's a decent person despite bad circumstances."

RYDER COULDN'T HELP but notice how many times Faith had mentioned that her little brother was a decent kid. Was she trying to convince him, or herself? As much as he doubted any McCabe son could be good, he would give Faith the benefit of the doubt. His trust was an entirely different story.

If he was going to help—and there was

no refusing now that he knew she was possibly pregnant with his child and there was the slightest chance of foul play—he needed more information. Besides, the faster he could help her find Nicholas, the sooner he'd be able to focus on what he really wanted to know more about—the baby she was carrying.

"You haven't spoken to his mother. There could be an easy explanation for all this, Faith," he said, ignoring the tension sitting like a wall between them.

Faith shook her head. "I didn't want her to know about our relationship. It would only cause more tension between the two of them and I doubt she'd welcome a McCabe anyway, considering my father hasn't stepped up to help her in any way. She can't be happy that he refused support, and I'm not saying that he's right but neither is sleeping with a married man."

"She may be able to clear this up in five minutes. We have to talk to her," he said plainly.

"After the way my father treated her I doubt she'll want to see anyone from his side of the family again." Faith made a harrumph sound.

"That may well be true. Doesn't mean we skip a step," he said. If one uncomfortable conversation could clear this up, so be it. "Besides, she can't be all that bad if Nicholas has turned out as well as you say."

"Fine. But Nicholas isn't close to his mother and he wouldn't tell her if he was in trouble."

"She may have filed a missing persons report. If she hasn't, we'll need her help since she's his legal guardian. How long did you say he's been gone?" he asked. Cooperation from Nicholas's mother would go a long way with the law. In fact, she'd have to be the person to officially report him missing.

"It's been three days," she said with a voice so weak Ryder's heart squeezed. He couldn't afford to let his emotions overrule logic this time. They'd had him thinking that getting mixed up with her was a good idea in the first place.

"I've been on campouts without cell service longer than that," he said, trying to offer what little reassurance he could under the circumstances.

Faith shot him a look.

"If his mother filed a report, three days would be enough time for law enforcement to take her seriously," he said. What if the kid ran away? From what Faith said the boy came from an unstable home. "There are other logical possibilities. Maybe he got impatient. Or he and his mother could've gotten into a fight and he's staying away while they both cool off. She might've done something that he didn't want to tell you about since you don't like her in the first place."

"I have to think he would've called me like he always does. And he's never missed a tutoring session." If that was true she made a good point.

"Maybe he figures you'll try to talk him into going home and he's not ready."

"It's a thought," she said without much enthusiasm, and he could tell she was going along with him even though her heart wasn't in it.

"There's another more likely possibility," he offered.

"And that is?" She was clicking through the possibilities with him, and he could tell from her subdued expression that nothing was sparking.

"He might've met a girl." He held his hand up when she started to speak. "Hold on. Hear me out. Fifteen-year-old boys are hormones on legs. It's possible that he hit it off with someone and is staying at her house for a few days."

Faith held up her cell phone.

"Last thing a hormonal teenager wants is the voice of reason in his ear. Believe me, I speak from experience," Ryder said. "We had a lot of those in our house over the years between the six of us boys."

"I'll take your word for it," she said. "I remember you at that age. And the need for an adrenaline rush hasn't dimmed, has it, Ryder?"

"I like to think I'm more mature now."

"I'd like to think I'm a supermodel," she jabbed back. That quick wit of hers still made him want to smile. This time, he resisted the urge.

He glanced at his watch. "It's late. I'll get coverage on the ranch tomorrow, so we can get started first thing in the morning. We'll start with his mother."

An emotion he couldn't put his finger on flashed in her eyes. Disappointment? Regret?

If Faith thought this was the beginning of the two of them bonding, working together as life partners, she was sorely mistaken.

THE HOUSE WAS SMALL, a two-bedroom bungalow with cars parked on the street and, in some cases, right on the front lawn. Those were on cinder blocks. There was a couch positioned on a porch or two instead of actual patio furniture. Chain-link fences surrounded mostly barren yards with patches of yellow grass. Ryder couldn't help but take note of the contrast to the McCabes' expansive ranch in Bluff.

Ryder parked in front of 622 Sycamore like Faith had instructed and cut the engine. They'd made small talk on the way over, mostly about the cold front that had blown through last night and the irony of this being the first day of spring when temps were barely hovering above freezing. In Texas, anything was possible when it came to the weather.

"What's her name?" Ryder nodded toward the house.

"Celeste Bowden," Faith supplied.

"Okay. Let's go talk to Celeste Bowden." He made a move for the door handle and stopped when a disgusted grunt sounded to his right.

"Fair warning, she's not going to be happy to see me," she said on a sigh.

"I already gathered that from our conversation last night." He shouldered the door of his cab open. "Does she love her son?"

"In her own way? Yes," Faith admitted.

He glanced around the neighborhood. "She may not take care of him in the way you'd like but she won't want anyone taking him from her. If she hasn't heard from him by now then she'll be worried. And that's the only shot we have at her talking to us, so keep a low profile and let me take the lead."

Ryder tried not to focus on the fact that he didn't sleep a wink last night, tossing and turning over the news that he might be a father. Two cups of black coffee first thing this morning had sharpened his mind.

Following closely behind Faith, he couldn't deny a new protectiveness he felt for her because of the child she was carrying. He still didn't know how to deal with the news other than to be stunned. Sleeping had been a nonissue. He kept waiting for the shock to wear off so he could figure out his next steps. He'd stayed at the fishing cabin last night, forcing down thoughts of the times he and Faith had spent there. Last night was the first time he'd been back to the place where too many memories could impact his judgment.

This morning, she'd left her car there and they'd decided to take his pickup, leaving long before sunrise. Conversation was a strain now, and he missed the easy way they used to talk to each other.

Ryder hopped the pair of concrete porch steps onto the small patio, and then opened the weathered screen door. It creaked and groaned. No way could anyone slip into this house quietly. And especially because a few dogs in neighboring yards fired off rapid barks. At this rate, the whole neighborhood would be up, trying to figure out what was going on. On second thought, he might need to talk to neighbors. Maybe it was good that they'd be up.

Ryder knocked on the wood part of the door. Most of the top half was glass. White paint chipped off the rest.

No answer.

This time, Ryder pounded on the door, rattling the glass in the window. The neighborhood dogs reacted again, going crazy barking as a figure moved toward the door. The woman came into view as she neared. Her hair wild, she wore jeans and a half-unbuttoned flannel shirt, no doubt the same clothes she had on last night. Worry lines and too much hard living shadowed what might have been an attractive face at one time.

"Who are you and what do you want?" she asked, cracking the door. Her gaze bounced from Ryder to Faith. Her eyes widened as she zeroed in on Faith, no doubt picking up on the fact that she was Hollister McCabe's daughter. "Never mind. You're not welcome here. Get off my porch."

Celeste tried to slam the door but Ryder stuck the toe of his boot inside to stop her. "I'm sorry to wake you, but we're here out of concern for your son. Is there any chance we can come inside?"

"No." Angry lines did nothing to improve the woman's hard features. On closer appraisal, she couldn't have been older than her midthirties.

"I know he hasn't been home. We just want to get some information so we can figure out where he is," Faith said.

"My son is none of your business." Celeste stared at Faith before giving Ryder a disgusted look. "Now move so I can close the door."

Bringing Faith might've been a mistake. Ryder shifted to the right a little in order to block a direct line of sight between the two of them.

"No need to do anything you'll regret," Ryder said quickly, trying to bring the focus back to him. "We're here to ask a few questions and then we'll be on our way."

"You with the law?" Celeste asked, glancing at the pocket of his jacket, most likely looking for a badge.

Ryder shook his head.

"Then let go of my door and get the hell off my property," Celeste ground out.

"But—" Faith started.

"Last time I checked, trespassing was against the law. If you're not gone by the time I count to three, I'm calling the cops." Celeste's tone intensified with her rising anger. Her gaze was locked onto Faith and he could tell that she was struggling to get past coming face-to-face with a McCabe.

"Okay." Ryder held his hands up in surrender and shifted his boot, allowing her to shut them out.

The woman slammed the door so hard he thought the glass might break. She took a step back, folded her arms and stared them down.

"I hope you won't let anything happen to your son because you're not thrilled with us. We want to work together to find him and make sure he's okay. We all know he wouldn't disappear like this without answering his cell," he said through the thin glass.

An emotion crossed her features, briefly softening her hard stare. She made a move for the door handle, but hesitated.

And then she shook her head.

Damn. He was so close to getting through to her.

"Did you eat breakfast this morning?" Ryder asked Faith. He spoke loud enough for Nicholas's mother to hear.

"What? No. Why?" Her brow knit in confusion.

"There's a diner in town." He turned and hopped off the porch.

"That's it?" Her voice outlined her shock as she stood rooted. "You're giving up just like that? And now you're hungry?"

"Get in the truck."

"But she might know something. I can't walk away without figuring out a way to make her talk to us."

"She won't. Not like this. She needs a minute to think it over. Besides, she's listening to us and watching every move we make." Ryder slowed but didn't turn; he kept right on walking.

"Then we should talk to the neighbors. Someone might've seen something. Don't tell me we drove all the way out here to eat breakfast." The desperation in her voice almost made him turn around. Almost.

"If you want her to help find Nicholas, get in the truck."

"Fine." Faith stomped so hard the earth should've cracked. The only thing that did was Ryder's face, in a grin. She still had that same fierce determination.

As soon as she took her seat and slammed the truck door closed, she whirled on him. "I hope this means you have a plan, because you just blew the only lead we have so far."

"I didn't but you almost did," he said, keeping that wry grin intact as he turned the key in the ignition. The engine fired up.

"Me?" She was so angry the word came out in a high-pitched croak. "You're joking, right?"

"Never been more serious." He navigated the pickup through the one-lane street. "And you should calm down. Getting upset can't be good for...*it*." He motioned toward her belly, not really sure what to call the baby yet.

"Well, then, you're going to have to explain everything to me as if I'm a two-year-old because I don't understand," she said, dodging his baby comment.

Chapter Three

Downtown Braxton, Texas, had a post office, a diner, a bank and a city hall. The diner was across the street from city hall and anchored an otherwise empty strip center. Ryder parked, fed the meter and then opened Faith's door for her.

"You still haven't told me what we're doing here," she said, taking his hand.

He ignored the frisson of heat where their fingers touched. Sexual chemistry wasn't the problem between them, never had been. Trust was, and it appeared to be an issue on both sides. As for him, there'd be no way to get around her deception and build any kind of bond. Yes, he was still angry at her, and that was why he didn't want to think about the attraction he felt or anything else that didn't directly impact finding Nicholas.

"She'll come and then she'll be ready to

talk," he said. "She needs a minute to come to terms with the fact that you care."

"How do you know that?" Faith didn't bother to hide her frustration; angry lines creased her forehead.

"Curiosity will get the best of her. She loves him. I could see it in her eyes. She wants to find him as much as we do, and we planted the seed that we're concerned," he clarified.

"I hope you're right," she said.

"She's also proud. She might not take care of him the way you would but that doesn't mean she doesn't love him. He might be the only family she has and she won't let go easily," he clarified.

"Celeste didn't get what she wanted from my dad. I figured she was just using him, maybe even got pregnant on purpose hoping for a free ride. But she kept Nicholas and has becn bringing him up ever since even though my dad was a jerk and refused to pay support," she said thoughtfully.

He didn't address the irony of that idea given their current situation, and she acknowledged that she was thinking the same thing with a quick flash of her eyes toward him. It was a good sign that she'd calmed down and could think through the situation clearly. Faith was smart.

"Oh, no." She suddenly stopped at the diner door, turned and ran toward the trash can.

"What is it?" he asked.

"This isn't good." She bent over and clutched her stomach. "I feel awful."

"Is it the baby?" Her expression made him worry that something might be truly wrong. A feeling of panic struck his chest faster than stray lightning and he was caught off guard by the jolt of fear that came with thinking something serious might be wrong.

"What can I do?" he asked as she emptied her stomach. He followed her and held her hair back from her face, helpless to offer any real comfort. He could see that her cheeks were flushed. The back of her neck was hot to the touch despite the frigid temps, so he swept her hair off her neck to cool her down, offering what little support he could.

"Sorry," she said before emptying another round into the trash can.

"Don't apologize for being sick. What do you need?" Watching her retch over a garbage bin made him wish he could do something to make it better. Anything besides just keep her neck cool. He'd never felt so useless in his life.

When she was finished, she glanced up at him looking embarrassed.

"Are you okay?" he asked.

"I should've skipped that cup of decaf I had this morning on an empty stomach." She leaned against a brick pillar next to the garbage can for support. "I'll be fine in a few minutes. It's probably just nerves."

She looked at him and must've seen the panic in his eyes.

"Promise. It'll pass. I went through worse than this in those first few months," she said.

"Hold on." He retrieved a bottle of water from the cab of his truck, unscrewed the lid and handed it to her. "Maybe this'll help."

She rinsed her mouth out before wetting a cloth and dabbing it on her face. "That's much better, actually. Thank you."

He shouldn't feel such a strong sense of satisfaction. He needed to be stockpiling reserves against that dam he'd built, tossing bags of sand against it for reinforcement, because seeing the way she looked a few moments ago had threatened to put a crack in a wall he couldn't afford to break.

An old two-door hatchback buzzed into the parking spot on the other side of Ryder's truck with Celeste behind the wheel.

"You're sure you're better?" he asked Faith, relieved that her color was returning.

"Yeah. Much. The cold weather is helping."

"Let's get inside before she sees us out here

and takes off. We have a better chance of getting her to open up if she can't easily hop into her car if you say anything to frustrate her."

Faith shot him a severe look.

"Hey, I'm just making sure she doesn't slam the door in our face again," he said, taking her arm. Holding on to her was a bad idea, especially while she seemed so vulnerable. He ignored the hammering against the fault line of the dam wall and the way his pulse picked up as he guided her inside the diner, chalking his reaction up to residual sexual chemistry. Even through her coat he felt the sizzle between them. "Table for two."

The place had about twenty tables in a dining space to the left and a counter with bar stools for quick service on his right. There were plenty of windows at the front and only a few customers. Most of whom were spread around at tables in the back.

"Sit anywhere you like," a waitress said from behind the counter. She was filling an old-fashioned soda glass from a spout.

Ryder motioned toward a booth in front near the half wall of windows, farthest away from anyone else in the hopes that Celeste would feel more comfortable talking. As it was, she looked ready to turn tail and run, and he couldn't afford to lose his only lead.

Faith was right earlier. They would circle back to talk to neighbors. He didn't expect to net much since no one had come outside to check on why the dogs were barking earlier. Even if someone had peeked from behind a curtain, they wouldn't talk. Celeste's was a neighborhood that minded its own business.

Faith took off her coat and laid it across the booth before taking a seat. Ryder didn't bother to remove his jacket.

The two of them had just sat down and gotten comfortable when Celeste walked inside. She made eye contact with Ryder almost immediately and he could see just how tentative her trust in either of them was. It didn't matter. She was there. And he'd dealt with enough injured and spooked animals over the years to know it was in his and Faith's best interest to tread lightly.

Celeste had thrown on a pair of yoga pants and a T-shirt underneath a long coat and furry boots. Her hair was piled on top of her head in a loose bun. She didn't look much older than his eldest brother, Dallas, now that she was cleaned up. Fifteen years ago, she would've been barely been twenty years old. Faith's father was a real jerk for taking advantage of someone so young and then leaving when she was in trouble. But then Hollister McCabe had never been known for his morals. His being a jerk was most likely for sport.

Ryder glanced at Faith's stomach as Celeste pulled a chair up to the booth, hoping the stress of the morning wasn't taking a toll. He also wanted to get some food inside her now that he knew she hadn't eaten breakfast. That couldn't be good for her or the baby.

The waitress popped over and asked for drink orders.

"Coffee for me." He looked at Celeste, who nodded. "Make that two. Can we get some water and toast for my friend?"

A quick look at Faith showed she appreciated the gesture. Thankfully, she'd taken his earlier warning seriously and seemed to realize that it was best to leave the talking up to him.

"You need menus?" the waitress asked.

"Yes," Ryder said. "And can we get a rush on that toast?"

The waitress disappeared, returning a minute later with drinks, menus and toast. She set everything down and then said she'd give them a minute. Celeste shifted in her seat a few times, looking ready to bolt at a loud noise.

"I wasn't going to show but I figured you asked about the diner loud enough so I could hear it on purpose in case I changed my mind about talking," she said, staring at the fork rolled in a paper napkin. She seemed conflicted about being there. "You seem like you want to help. And I'm starting to get real worried about my boy."

Ryder nodded, letting her take the lead. He'd learned a long time ago that when someone was making an effort, it wasn't smart to get in their way.

"First off, I don't trust anyone with the last name McCabe." She glanced toward Faith, who was nibbling on her toast.

"I don't, either, if it makes you feel better," Ryder said, not bothering to mask his disdain for the McCabe family.

Celeste cocked her head sideways.

"I'm here to help find your son and I still haven't exactly figured out how I was talked into it," he said honestly. There was no reason to lie to the woman, and he figured they'd get further if he gained Celeste's trust.

"Since you showed up with a McCabe, I have to ask why you care about what happens to my boy."

"Faith and I have history. She's worried about Nicholas and couldn't go to her father. I'm not exactly thrilled to be here, but I couldn't walk away from someone asking for my help, either."

"Okay then." She must've picked up on the tension between him and Faith because she shot another contemptuous look toward Faith.

"We might not want it for the same reasons, but we all want the same thing. To find Nicholas and bring him home safely," Ryder said. "It doesn't matter why."

Celeste nodded. Her shoulders slumped forward and she looked completely wrung out. "I didn't sleep last night from worry. At first I thought he found a girl and ran off."

"He wouldn't do that," Faith said a little too intensely.

"How would you know?" Celeste said with disdain.

Faith suddenly became interested in the tabletop. "I know my brother."

A noise tore from Celeste's throat. "You don't know fifteen-year-old boys."

"Nicholas isn't like that," Faith said, her defenses rattled. Her reaction was putting Celeste on edge, and that wasn't going to get them what they wanted: her cooperation.

"I can remember a few times when I did stupid stuff at that age. Hormones and a still-developing brain don't exactly make the best combination," Ryder intervened with a warning look toward Faith.

Celeste angled her body toward him, effectively closing Faith out of the conversation. "My point exactly. He's a good boy but that don't mean nothing when it comes to teenage hormones. That's what I thought three days ago. Now, I don't know. It ain't like him not to call. He's never done that before."

"What about his actions in the days leading up to his…" He didn't want to say the word *disappearance*. "Had he been staying out later than usual?" Ryder hoped to cash in on her conspiratorial feelings.

"Not that I know of," she said with a tentative glance toward Faith. "I work nights but he's always there by the time I get home the next morning."

"What time is that usually?" Ryder asked, nodding his head. Celeste was holding something back. What?

"There's no set time," she said.

"Bar closes at two o'clock," Faith said, scorn in her tone. "Nicholas said she doesn't come home until the next morning and sometimes until lunch."

Ryder shot her one of his you're-not-helping looks and then refocused on Celeste.

"Was he hanging out with any new people or had his behavior at school changed recently?" Ryder pressed. "Any notes or calls from the counselor?"

"None. No new people, either. At least none that I know of, but then boys don't exactly tell their mothers every little detail," she said after a thoughtful pause and a long hard look at Faith.

"What about his cell phone?" he asked. "I'm sure you've tried calling. Texting? I'm guessing there's been no response."

"None. And I haven't seen or heard it since he left. Figured he took it with him. That thing goes everywhere with him, including the bathroom."

"Did you search his bedroom for it?" Faith asked, looking determined to get her two cents in. Ryder had never been able to control her, and maybe that was the point. Maybe she was showing him that she was the one who should be in charge. Or maybe it was genuine concern for her little brother, a brother who'd been abandoned by her side of the family and who needed her help. Either way, her talking wasn't a good thing. If he'd known her presence would cause this much of a stir with Celeste, he would've come alone.

He took a sip of his black coffee while Celeste shot Faith a sour look.

Celeste fished out her cell phone, entered a password onto the screen and pulled up her message history. "Look, he makes me text him every night to make sure I got in my car safe. No one's ever done that for me before. Plus, he hasn't tried to get a hold of me using anyone else's phone, either." She flashed her eyes at Faith. "I know my Nicholas is a good boy but even the nice ones get mixed up in the wrong crowd sometimes. That's what I figured happened when he didn't respond to my text three nights ago. It's not like him to stay away this long, and that has me figuring he's done something he shouldn't. Something real ba—"

"He wouldn't—" Faith started to say, but Ryder shushed her.

"Let her finish," he said with a look that said this would all be over if she kept pressing her agenda. Nicholas's mother was talking to them, and Faith needed to cool it.

Celeste pulled a piece of paper out of her purse and flattened it on the table.

"Look there. Doesn't seem like you know Nicholas as much as you claim to." She fired the accusation directly at Faith.

It was a note from Nicholas, saying that it was his mother's turn to wait up for him and wonder where he was for a change.

Faith's face went blank.

"Can I see that?" Faith asked.

Celeste didn't immediately move.

"Please. Just for a second," Faith said, softer this time.

The woman relented.

Faith took the paper and then studied the words as she traced her finger around the shapes.

"Nicholas didn't write that." She folded her arms with that indignant look on her face again. Before Ryder could remind her that she wasn't helping, she scooted back in her seat.

"Well, it has his name right there." Celeste pointed to his signature.

"I don't care what it says. I've done homework with him a thousand times and that's not his handwriting," Faith said matter-of-factly. The shaming quality to her tone wasn't going to help matters.

"When have you been here to help Nicholas with anything?" Celeste leaned back in her chair, got another sour look on her face like she'd just sucked on a pickle.

"All the time," Faith shot back, ignoring the warning look Ryder was giving her.

"That's it. I'm done here." Celeste pushed off the table and stood.

Ryder popped to his feet, too.

"Don't leave. I'm just worried about Nicholas," Faith defended.

That was all it took for Celeste to snatch her keys out of her purse and then head for the door.

The waitress appeared as Ryder took off after the distraught woman.

Faith made a move to follow.

"Don't you dare get up. Order food. I'll try to clean up your mess," he barked.

Celeste revved the engine, one hand gripping the steering wheel as she craned her neck to check for clearance. She was ready to gun it and get the heck out of there as Ryder jogged up to her window, hoping he could perform some major damage control.

"She doesn't mean to come off that way," he said, startling her.

"I don't need no one judging my life and especially one of Hollister's snot-nosed kids. She doesn't know what me and Nicholas have gone through because her SOB of a father wouldn't support us," Celeste said through a sneer.

"No, she doesn't. And you're one hundred percent right about Hollister McCabe. I can't stand that family personally," Ryder agreed. "There's no excuse for him abandoning you and Nicholas."

"Then what are you doing with one of 'em?" She put the car in Park but didn't take her foot off the brake.

"I was honest before. She came to me asking for my help," he said. "Before you think I'm some Good Samaritan, I turned her down."

"How come you showed up here anyway?"

"I believed her when she said Nicholas was a good boy. I won't try to convince you that she's better than her family, but I know you'll understand that because of who her father is she had nowhere else to turn but me."

Celeste stared out her windshield, didn't move. That was a good sign.

"She's been sneaking Nicholas money for years, even though getting caught would end her relationship with her father. Hollister McCabe doesn't care if someone's flesh and blood if they cross him, as I'm sure I don't have to tell you," he said.

"Now that she's turned up I figured it had to be her giving my Nicholas money all these years," she admitted.

"It's money out of her pocket. Her father doesn't know," he said. "And she needs to keep it that way."

"I don't give two hoots about her family problems," Celeste said, searching out a pack of cigarettes from the dashboard. She pulled out a smoke and lit it. "You want one?"

Ryder shook his head.

"I'm not saying she's perfect, believe me. She cares about Nicholas, though. And if he is in trouble, he can use all the help he can get no matter whose last name is attached. Don't you think?"

That seemed to strike a chord. She twisted the cigarette around her fingers.

"If you know anything that can help find your son, I'd appreciate you telling me. I understand why you don't like Faith and I won't argue against your points, but I'm not the enemy. I'm only here because Nicholas could be in trouble, and if that's the case we need to work together."

"You don't think he's with a girl? Now that I think about it, that Swanson chick was hanging around our place an awful lot before he took off," Celeste said, taking a long drag. A smoke cloud broke around her face as she blew twin plumes out of her nostrils.

"Maybe. If he's as good a kid as the two of you say he'd let you know where he is. Has he ever stayed away overnight?"

"No. Never. He worries too much about me. He won't even sleep over anyone's house because he wants to be home for me." Celeste took another drag off her smoke and stared out the windshield. A few tears trickled down her cheeks. She quickly wiped them away and took another pull. "I didn't come home the other night. I thought maybe that's why he took off. Then I found the letter. He's been threatening me with that one for years so I guess I had it coming."

"You haven't reported him missing?" Ryder asked, noting that if someone had kidnapped Nicholas they didn't want to raise suspicion right away. Another bad sign as far as Ryder was concerned. This must've been targeted and someone was buying time. Ryder wouldn't allow himself to go down the road that said they were already too late.

She shook her head.

"Then let me help you find him."

Celeste flicked her cigarette out the window, taking care to miss Ryder. He crushed the butt under the heel of his boot.

"I'll stop by the sheriff's office and see what he says," she relented.

"That's a good start. Ask him about an Amber Alert and see if he's willing to go there. What about friends?" Ryder pressed.

"He kept to himself mostly." She shrugged. "There was one boy who always came around. His name's Kyle. He's the Sangers' boy."

"You have his address?"

"No." She shook her head for emphasis. "I'm not too good with writing stuff like that down. Nicholas said he lives in the pink siding house two streets over."

"I'm sure we'll be able to find it," he offered, thinking there couldn't be too many houses with pink siding in the neighborhood.

"I never did catch your name," Celeste said.

"Ryder O'Brien."

Her eyes widened at hearing his last name. It was a common reaction and usually benefited Ryder.

"Nicholas is a good kid. Can you bring him home?" she asked.

"That's the goal."

"He ain't never been in trouble." A desperate sigh slipped out before Celeste could quash it and regain her composure. She looked like the kind of person who hadn't had many breaks in life. She obviously cared about her son, and Ryder couldn't help but feel sorry for the situation McCabe had put her in.

"I know she's going about it all wrong, but Faith cares a lot about Nicholas," Ryder said, testing the water. Maybe he could smooth things over a little between her and Faith. Convince Faith that it would be better for Nicholas if she made an effort with his mother. Besides,

Faith seemed to have genuine feelings for her half brother, and she would need all the family she could rally around her when her parents learned that she was carrying his child. He'd almost like to be a fly on the wall of that conversation just to see Hollister McCabe's reaction. And even if Faith wasn't worried about losing the support of her father, Ryder knew her well enough to realize that she wouldn't want to alienate her mother. Faith had always felt protective of her mother, and especially since the woman had started depending on so many pills to get her through the day.

"My boy is none of her business." Celeste's lips turned into a sneer, a chilly response.

"Understood. I just wanted you to know she has just as many issues with her father as you and she's carrying a secret that will cause him to turn his back on her, too," Ryder added.

"That's impossible on both counts," Celeste said, her tone flat. "I want nothing to do with him or his family."

"He's no friend of mine, either," Ryder said. "I'm on your side."

"I appreciate your help but I don't have no money—"

"None's necessary," he cut her off. "This is for Nicholas. If something happened to him, we'll figure it out and bring him home."

Celeste wiped a stray tear.

"You have a pen? I want to give you my number in case he makes contact." Ryder pulled out the business card of his family's lawyer, wishing he'd thought to have some of his own printed.

Celeste searched around in her car and in the glove box. "Afraid not."

"Hold on. I'll grab one from inside," he said.

She nodded.

He jogged into the restaurant and to the counter. He still had a long way to go to gain Celeste's trust but he'd made progress. "There a pen I can borrow?"

"Sure thing. Should be one right over there." The waitress motioned toward the register.

Ryder thanked her as he located the blue Bic pen. He scribbled his name and number on the back of the card before turning toward the all-glass door. He stopped and issued a frustrated grunt.

Celeste was gone.

Chapter Four

"I can't keep running interference between you and Nicholas's mother," Ryder said, taking his seat at the table. Anger stewed behind his dark eyes and he wore a disgusted expression. "Finish breakfast and I'll take you home."

"I'm sorry." Faith meant it, too.

Ryder's shoulders were bunched. The muscle in his jaw ticked. He was done.

She really hadn't intended to insult Nicholas's mother even though the woman needed a few stern lessons in parenting. Hormones were hell. "Meeting her had an unexpected effect on me and I promise not to let my emotions take over next time."

He gave her the glare that left no room for doubt that there wouldn't be a repeat because she was on her own.

"Ryder, please. I'm begging. I'll handle

people however you tell me to if you'll give me another chance."

"Where was this attitude ten minutes ago when it would've made a difference?" he shot back, but the hard lines on his forehead were already softening.

"Not where it should've been. I admit." She'd gained a little ground, but he wasn't exactly happy with her yet.

He picked up his fork and stabbed it into his eggs. Another good sign.

"Well, keep it in check next time because we need her and you probably just pushed her away." The bite didn't make it into his mouth before he continued, "No. You know what. You asked me here and then made it next to impossible to gain her cooperation."

"That's not entirely true. I didn't ask you to bring me to her. I already told you that she can't help us. Or won't." As soon as the tart words left her mouth, she regretted them. She put her hands up in the surrender position. "I didn't mean that, either. I don't know what's wrong with me except that every single emotion I've ever had is at full tilt these past few months." She didn't even want to talk about the crazy changes going on inside her body, changes that weren't visible to others and yet she was keenly aware of her hips starting to expand and her belly having a little pooch. Then, there were the hormones.

"Take it easy." His tone was meant to calm her down. His look of pity made her feel even more frustrated at how fragile she must seem. That didn't go over well. Concern was one thing. Pity was something altogether different. Faith wasn't helpless.

"I want to reassure you that I can have an adult conversation without putting people off. That woman… Nicholas's mother…gets under my skin. I mean Nicholas had it tough enough without a father around and then she adds to his stress and…confusion by making him responsible for her. He's just a kid and he doesn't deserve any of this battle going on between people who are supposed to be grown adults."

Ryder caught her gaze and held it as he folded his hands and placed them against the edge of the table.

"You make a lot of good points about her situation and I can't help but see the similarities to ours," he said. "We're going to need to learn to work together so our differences don't affect our child."

Faith took in a breath.

"And you might not like what I have to say but you need to hear it anyway. As far as I can see, she's the only parent the boy has who loves him. Some kids don't even get that much and he's damn lucky to have someone in his life who cares about him. Which leads to my second point. Nicholas has two."

Faith knew Ryder well enough to know better than to argue his points, and especially because they stung. The hard truth had a way of doing that when someone was being too stubborn to see it. And Faith could admit to being at fault there.

Besides, Ryder would've seen the damage firsthand that neglected children deal with and could probably recite the statistics on what happened to them because of his and his mother's generous work with children's charities. He'd said that she'd been the inspiration for him and his brothers to become more involved in the community. Ryder might like to push the boundaries in his personal life, but he also was smart enough to appreciate the privileges he'd been given growing up an O'Brien and he was decent enough to want to help others.

"We might disagree about his mother but you're right about one thing. My brother will always have me," she defended. She stopped him from going down the neglected child road with Nicholas.

"It's not the same as a mother or father being present and you know it." His voice was a frustrating sea of calm.

"Why not? I probably should've petitioned the courts years ago. I'm old enough now and I have plenty of money to fight for him." Ryder was striking a chord of truth and it grated on her.

"Which your father would cut off the second he knew you were involved with his bastard son." The words were harsh and she knew that he'd used that term to shock her. It was exactly what her father would call Nicholas. And no matter how much it pained her to admit, her father would see this as black-and-white. She had to think that there was still decency in him, but that part of her was shrinking, especially since she had to confront the reality of the way she feared he'd treat her when he learned of her pregnancy.

"Let me put this to you another way," Ryder said.

"I'm listening," she said, doing her best to calm the tremors in her arms. Hormones made her body do crazy things, not the least of which was shaking when she got angry or nervous.

"Have you ever asked Nicholas if he wanted

to leave his mother?" His voice was a study in calmness.

"I don't have to. I see how she treats him with my own eyes," she fired back, her defenses on high alert.

"You just made my point. You can't do what's best for a teenager without actually consulting with him to find out what he really wants. He may not think he needs what you're offering and you might end up pushing him further away with your good intentions," Ryder said, and he was making more sense than she wanted to admit.

Faith wouldn't share the fact that she'd been plotting and secretly saving money for years. Her father was watchful of her finances. She wasn't crazy enough to think that her father's good will would last forever. She had an overseas account—a safety net—that she'd been building for her and Nicholas. She might actually have to use it now in order to protect her own child. Her father would cut her off in every way possible and freeze her personal accounts the minute he heard the news about the baby. She had no job outside of working for the family, and so he could easily cut off her livelihood. Faith couldn't imagine that her mother would stand up to the man, not even on her behalf. Her mother wasn't strong like

Faith and she had always issued her mother a free pass in that department. The pregnancy was starting to give Faith a new perspective. She could acknowledge that she felt even more protective of Nicholas. Ryder's words hit her full force. Was she being unrealistic in thinking that she could make better decisions for Nicholas than he could make on his own? Or worse, had she turned into her father?

The realization startled her because she knew firsthand how stifling it was to have other people make her decisions. What she was thinking was no different. What a slap in the face that thought was. Ryder was being logical while she was being fueled by sentiment.

"My hormones make me feel like every emotion I have is on steroids and I may have taken some of that out on his mother," she admitted. The truth left a bitter taste in her mouth. "I know you understand the need to take care of your own, Ryder. I've seen your relationship with your brothers, especially with Joshua, and how well you take care of family. Surely you can at least see where I'm coming from."

Ryder didn't immediately pick up his fork. He just sat there staring at the food, contemplating what she'd said, and that was the best that she could ask for.

"Under the circumstances, I can see where you'd feel overprotective of Nicholas," he finally said. "While I don't have a lot of experience with pregnant women, we've had a baby boom at the ranch and I can see how different my brothers are now. They're more defensive of everyone and everything around them. I'm sure it's primal. Nature's way of taking care of these helpless little creatures. But it's a fine line to becoming overbearing and one you don't want to cross."

"Point taken." She paused a beat. "I heard about Dallas, Tyler and Joshua. I don't even know where to start. Congratulations to all of them." Three out of six O'Brien men were engaged and in settled relationships in various stages of wedding planning, or so she'd heard. Her direct line into that family had been severed when she'd been forced to walk away from Ryder.

"The ranch has turned into a kid farm," he said with a laugh, his easy O'Brien charm returning—that same charm that caused a thousand butterflies to take flight in her stomach.

"Is that a bad thing?" She couldn't read him when it came to his feelings toward kids.

"No. Not for my brothers. They seem happier than they've ever been. Maybe that's why I'm feeling tenderhearted right now, so I'll let it slide that you basically ran off our only real connection to what might've happened to Nicholas." He wasn't exactly offering forgiveness, but she'd take what she could get from him under the circumstances and be grateful for the progress. Ryder was back on board and he was speaking to her.

"If you're being honest with yourself—" he held his hands up in the surrender position "—and I can tell you've been taking this seriously, then you have to consider the possibility that your father might be involved."

"I wondered how long it would take you to get to that accusation. For a minute, I didn't think you'd stoop that low." A bolt of anger shot lightning-quick down her spine as she remembered just how much Ryder disliked her family.

"It's worth considering," he defended.

"Not to me, it isn't," she said.

"What makes you so sure he's not involved?"

"First of all, my father might be a cheating jerk, which makes him a scumbag and bad husband, but he'd never hurt one of his own," she said, her pulse rising as she defended him. Granted, her father wasn't father-of-the-year material but she hated how easy it was for Ryder to sling that accusation. This situation was back to the McCabes being the bad guys.

"Unless he doesn't consider Nicholas part of the fold. In which case, he wouldn't give a hoot what happened to him, and I doubt Celeste would give us information about any recent exchanges she's had with him if there have been any," Ryder said calmly.

"Nicholas is as much of a McCabe as I am whether anyone wants to acknowledge him or not," she cried, voice rising.

"To you. Maybe. To your father..." He rolled his shoulders and his right brow shot up.

"He wouldn't do something like this," she repeated, and she had to believe it was true.

"While I'm digging around I plan to investigate every angle. And that's one." He set his fork down, signaling that he was done with breakfast.

"Where to next?" she asked stiffly. She should've seen this coming. It always came down to this, to the fact that the McCabes were horrible people. Granted, it didn't help that her father and brothers seemed eager to support that notion. She brought her hand to rest on her belly. Not all McCabes were horrible people.

Ryder motioned toward her plate. "We don't go anywhere until you finish eating."

RYDER PULLED IN front of the only house with pink siding in a three-block radius of Celeste's place in either direction. It was similar to hers, bungalow-style and in the same neighborhood a few streets over just as Celeste had said.

"Let me take the lead," he said to Faith, who'd been quiet on the ride over, and he hoped that she was seriously considering what he'd said. Without a doubt, Hollister McCabe could be involved and if not directly then indirectly. He knew that she couldn't exactly ask her father outright without giving away the fact that she'd been in touch with Nicholas all these years. None of which would matter to her if she truly believed that her father wasn't involved and/or would be willing to help.

"Okay. I won't say a word." She held up her hands trying to mimic the Scout's honor pledge. Her eyes tried so desperately to convey sincerity.

It shouldn't make him laugh. He recovered quickly.

"You better take this seriously," he warned.

She rolled her eyes at him. "Like I wouldn't. I was trying to show you that I'm not just a raging head case."

"Keep the hormones in check and we'll get answers faster. *Hormones in check.* That's your mantra," he said as flatly as he could. It wouldn't do either one of them any good to get too comfortable. Once this was over, they were going to have a sit-down about the pregnancy and Ryder's role in his child's life. Working together given their current state of mistrust wouldn't be easy, but he was seeing firsthand just how important it would be to get along for their child's sake and he was willing to make a few concessions to ensure that happened.

"Got it." The amusement left her brown eyes and he did his best not to let it affect him. She was only doing what he said, taking this seriously and showing that she wouldn't do anything to get in the way of their investigation.

Ryder ushered her to the door of 225 Oak Drive, which had a similar wood and glass door combination as Nicholas's house except this one had a shade so he couldn't see inside. There was no screen door at this address. He figured he had a better chance of a person answering if they saw a woman standing there rather than a grown man, so he put Faith front and center while he moved off to the side.

Three knocks went unanswered.

"We can come back," he said, realizing it was close to eight o'clock in the morning and probably too early for anyone in the house to be awake and moving.

"Wouldn't Kyle have to get up for school?" she asked.

"Good point. Maybe he already left. I have no idea when kids have to be at school," Ryder said as he heard movement coming from inside. "Hold on."

The door cracked open and a smiling teen with tousled hair blinked his eyes open. Disappointment caused him to frown when he opened the door wide enough to see Ryder. "My aunt's not here."

Ryder nudged Faith, trying to communicate the message that she should take the lead.

"Are you Kyle?" Faith asked.

"Yeah," he said, leaning against the door. And then a scared-doe look passed behind his eyes and he stiffened. "Are you truant officers or something? It's not even time for school yet."

"No, believe me, it's nothing like that. I'm trying to find Nicholas Bowden. Have you seen him around?" she asked.

Recognition dawned. "Oh, you know Nicholas? Yeah, he's a friend of mine. I haven't seen him in like…forever."

"Do you remember how many days it's been?" she asked. "Two? Three?"

"It was last weekend, so, like, what...three days."

"Are you two close?" she asked. "Is it normal for you to go that long without talking?"

"Is Nicholas in trouble or something?" Kyle asked. A worry line dented his forehead.

"No, nothing like that," Ryder interjected when Faith seemed to blank on an excuse. He put his arm around her waist, ignoring the fizz of energy that came with touching her. "We're related, well, she is. We're driving through town and his mom thought you might've seen Nicholas. He's not picking up his cell."

The teen's expression morphed as he tossed his head back. "Got it. No. I haven't seen Nicholas for three days, maybe more. Not since he and Hannah starting getting hot and heavy. He hasn't been returning my texts, either."

"Hannah?"

"Yeah, she's some chick we met, well, *he* met, while we were hanging out down at Wired." He glanced from Faith to Ryder like they should know what that meant. "It's a place where they host LAN parties."

They looked at each other blankly.

"Come on. You don't know what a LAN

party is?" he whined, sounding every bit the teenager that he was.

"Afraid not," Faith said with a smile and a shrug.

"It's a gaming thing." He brought his hands up in the air and moved them like he was typing on a keyboard. "Computers."

"We'll take your word for it," Faith said with the same smile that had been right on target at melting Ryder's reservations about the two of them dating. He didn't want to admit just then how much that smile played a role in his attraction to her. Her bright eyes, intelligence and sense of humor had been a welcome surprise, considering all his preconceived notions about her. She'd been quiet in school and he could admit now that he'd believed she was stuck on herself, which couldn't have been more off base. His experience with McCabes came from knowing her brothers. Once he got to know her, he realized just how wrong he'd been. Faith and her brothers were polar opposites. Ryder had had a few run-ins with Jason, the youngest. That kid had been born ready to fight. O'Briens didn't start trouble. They didn't back away from it, either. If trouble was stupid enough to snare one of them, the response came in the form of six angry brothers. McCabes had never been good at math or anything else that required using the head put on their shoulders as far as Ryder could tell. So when he'd run into Faith near the fishing cabin and they started spending time together, he'd been most surprised at her intelligence and wit, which had only made her more beautiful. The fact that he'd felt lost and alone at the time, with darkness all around him, had drawn him to her light even more.

Kyle also seemed to notice her looks, because the kid was standing there beaming at her. It shouldn't grate on Ryder's nerves as much as it did.

"You know where the girl you mentioned lives?" Ryder interrupted.

"Sorry. Can't help you." The kid's eyes never left Faith.

"What about her cell number or social media?" Ryder asked.

"Sorry." Kyle shook his head. "This was the first time I'd seen her, and she went for my friend."

Ryder understood the logic. Kyle wouldn't try to connect with her after his friend got together with her, which didn't help their investigation in the least.

"How about you? You got a cell?" Ryder asked, and he was starting to get annoyed. He suppressed the urge to put his arm around

Faith's shoulders and show the kid just how far she was out of his league. It was stupid and childish. Ryder knew that on some level. But primal urge had him needing to keep everyone from the male species away from her. He lied to himself and said it was because she was carrying his child. That he was protective of the baby, and not territorial about her.

"Uh, yeah. Sure. Hold on." The kid disappeared and then returned a minute later. He'd wet his hair and run a quick comb through it. Now that made Ryder crack a smile. *She's way out of your league, kid. And not even when you get hair on your chest will she give a second look.*

Being stunning had never been Faith's problem. All the good looks in the world couldn't replace honesty or the fact that her last name was McCabe—and everything that brought along with it. Not that Ryder had minded the second part once he got past the initial surprise that she was nothing like her family. Sure, there'd been a burst of adrenaline from being with someone he knew better than to want at first. But that had died the second he got to know her and started having real feelings for her. Real feelings? They'd sure felt like it based on the sting he felt when she walked away.

And she'd rewarded him by returning when she needed him for something. He hadn't pegged her for the manipulative type. Like his dad had always said, "When people show you who they really are, believe them."

He could be objective about Nicholas, whereas Faith couldn't. Knowing that her brother had met a girl changed his thoughts about what might be happening.

"Where was the LAN party?" Ryder asked.

"At Marcus's place on Lone Oak. It's called Wired and it's about ten to fifteen minutes from here," Kyle said.

"Can you describe Hannah?" Faith seemed to catch on.

"Wow, yeah, she's a knockout. Black hair, brown eyes and—" he glanced from Faith to Ryder "—you know, great bod."

"And she's fifteen?" Based on Faith's frown, Hannah didn't match the type she thought her brother would go for.

Kyle shrugged and shot a look like *why would she ask that question?*

"Will you let us know if you hear from him?" Ryder asked. This interview was a dead end. Ryder exchanged cell numbers with the kid and walked Faith back to the truck.

"That was a bust," Faith said as soon as Ryder took his seat.

"We're certain there's a girl involved now. We didn't know that before," he said. That information would change things for Ryder if it hadn't been for the forged note.

"His mother mentioned a girl but it must not be the same one since his friend has no idea who she is. Where does that leave us?" she asked on a frustrated sigh.

"Speaking of Celeste, I want to circle back and drop my cell number in her mailbox. She needs to have a way to contact us if she hears anything."

"Good idea," Faith said.

"We might find out more about the girl if we hang around Wired," he said.

"It's a waste of time pursuing her. Nicholas would've told me if he liked someone," she said on a sharp sigh.

"You sure about that?" Ryder had his doubts.

And his mind kept circling back to her family being involved in the disappearance. He just couldn't put his finger on why or how.

Yet.

Chapter Five

The business front of Wired was the enclosed front porch of a house on the outskirts of town. The lots were a good acre in size, so there was plenty of distance between neighbors. A pair of compact cars were parked on the side of the house in tandem. Ryder parked on the street to make sure he didn't get blocked in. Although he doubted there'd be a rush when it opened at noon. The place gave new meaning to the words *small business*. There was a closed sign hanging on the screen door but he could see activity inside.

"Act like we know what we're doing," Ryder said to Faith as she took in the place. Her wide honey-brown eyes told him she was learning something else new about her brother. That gnawing feeling returned, and Ryder kept circling back to her family.

He opened the screen door and instructed her to stay close behind him.

A sallow-cheeked guy who couldn't be a day older than twenty was parked behind a desk, his gaze fixed on the screen in front of him.

"Hold on," he said without looking up. His chair was balanced on the back legs as he swished a mouse back and forth on an oversize pad and made barely audible grunting noises.

There were a couple of kids hunkered over a keyboard in one corner. A few open computers were dotted around the small room. There wasn't much in the way of decor, a few folding tables with poker chairs tucked underneath. The walls were covered with gaming posters announcing the next big release.

Sallow Cheeks cursed before tossing the mouse to the side. "So close to winning that one. What can I—" The second his eyes connected with Ryder and Faith, he froze.

"We're not cops, if that's what you're worried about," Ryder said, assuming that most kids were going to confuse them with people in positions of authority. There was no question that they looked out of place at Wired.

Sallow Cheeks regained his composure. "Oh, no. Didn't think you were. Besides, I run a legit business." He waved his right arm toward a framed permit hanging on the wall behind him. Ryder couldn't fault the kid for making money.

"She's looking for a relative. We were told he comes in here sometimes," Ryder continued, forging ahead.

Faith fingered the screen on her cell phone and then held it out toward Sallow Cheeks.

"I'm Marcus, by the way," he said, pushing hair off his forehead as he squinted at the picture of Nicholas.

Ryder introduced both himself and Faith.

"Yeah, I've seen that kid before. He doesn't come around much. He has a friend. What's his name?" He tapped his knuckles on the desk.

"Is it Kyle?" Faith asked.

"Right. Kyle usually swings by on Friday nights. He's brought this dude before."

"Nicholas Bowden?" Ryder asked.

"I guess." Marcus shrugged. "The kid was kind of quiet, you know. Mostly hung in the background when Kyle showed up to play."

"Do you remember the last time he was in? Nicholas?" Faith asked.

"A week ago." Marcus glanced at his computer screen. "Maybe two?"

"Was he with a girl?" Faith continued.

Marcus rocked his head and his eyes went wide. "Hannah."

"Do you know her?" Faith asked.

"She just started coming in a few weeks ago. Never saw her before that," Marcus said.

"You don't have an address for her, do you?" Ryder asked, wondering what a knockout, as Kyle had described her, would be doing hanging around with tech geeks. And there was no other explanation for hanging out at a place like Wired other than being a bona fide computer nerd.

"Nah." Marcus leaned backward, balancing on the back two legs of his chair.

"No credit card record?" Ryder asked.

"I wouldn't be able to give that to you anyway, dude. But, no, a girl like that doesn't usually have to pay her own way if you know what I mean."

"Are girls like Hannah common around here?" Ryder asked, figuring he already knew the answer but needed to check anyway.

"Nah. It would be nice, though," Marcus said.

"When was the last time you saw her?" A look crossed Faith's features that Ryder couldn't exactly pinpoint.

"Not since that kid was in. They paired up and left together. Haven't seen either one around since," he said. "But that's not really saying much. He wasn't a regular."

"This might sound like an odd question, but do you remember who was doing the picking up?" Ryder asked, and that netted a strange look from Faith.

Marcus nodded with a wink toward Ryder. "Definitely her. And that's probably why I remember it so clearly. I mean, she was hot and he was okay if you know what I mean." He shot an apologetic look toward Faith when she frowned.

"I hear you." A guy would notice something like that. "If you happen to see him, would you mind asking him to call his sister? He's probably caught up with this new girl and just forgot to check in with her, but she's worried."

Marcus nodded with a knowing look that said it wasn't the first time he'd received that kind of request. "I'll let him know if he shows up here."

"Thanks a lot." Ryder offered a handshake before escorting Faith outside.

Neither spoke until they reached the truck.

"I can't believe Nicholas has been there and never mentioned it," she finally said after buckling in.

Ryder could see where that detail might still

be on her mind. However, he'd locked onto something else. "She targeted him."

"What do you mean?"

Ryder put the gearshift in Drive and rolled the wheel left with his palm, guiding his pickup onto the street. He banked a U-turn at the next driveway. "She came on to Nicholas, not the other way around."

"He's a good-looking kid," she defended.

"Hear me out." Ryder located the highway and followed the GPS's instructions. "I get that Nicholas is nice-looking. He's also fifteen and full of hormones. He'd be attracted to any pretty girl who walked in front of him."

"Sounds pretty Neanderthal when you put it like that but, yes, I'm sure he is a normal, healthy fifteen-year-old boy," she said, her arms folded across her chest.

"So, let's think this through for a minute, because while Nicholas might still be young I don't get the impression this Hannah is his age and certainly not as innocent."

"What are you suggesting?"

"That there might be a reason a girl so out of his league became interested in him," he said, guiding them back onto Main Street.

It dawned on Faith. "She was some kind of decoy to get him alone so someone could snatch him."

"Once she isolated him, he could be kidnapped a helluva lot easier and everyone would think that he'd run off with a pretty girl," Ryder said. Between that and the note, someone was going to great lengths to buy time. "And the question should be why? Why would Nicholas be a target? What purpose would it serve? The first thing that comes to mind is money."

"Maybe someone figured out he's a McCabe and has contacted my father for ransom," Faith said, catching on to the theory. "That note wasn't his handwriting.

"It's not like I can ask my father outright. Hannah might be the key to finding Nicholas," she added. "Where do we start looking? Marcus back there doesn't know who she is, and neither did Kyle."

Ryder one-handed the steering wheel. "Can you access your father's email or desk?"

"Ryder." The distress in her voice had him taking his eyes off the road long enough for a quick glance at her. She was bent forward, holding her stomach.

"What's wrong?" he asked. He was already looking for an exit.

She must've picked up on his worry because she added, "Sick." Her hand came over her mouth.

"Hold on the best you can until I can get off the road," he said.

"Gas station," she managed to get out with a dry heave.

Ryder navigated onto the service road, and got to a Valu-X gas station pronto.

He'd barely come to a stop when her door flew open and she hopped out, bolting toward the little patch of grass near the service road. Bent over, she heaved as he pulled her hair from her face and rubbed her back. He wasn't cut out for feeling helpless.

"What can I do?" he asked when she finally straightened up.

"Water would be nice. And maybe some crackers," she said, and he didn't like how small and vulnerable her voice had become. He was used to strong and fiery Faith. These changes must be part of the hormones she'd talked about earlier. If so, he had a lot to learn about pregnant women, because he intended to help her through this and the next four months until the baby was born.

"I'll see what they have," he said. "Will you be all right?"

"Yeah." Her face was sheet white.

"Is it normally this bad?" he asked.

"It's much better than it was. Any little thing upsets my stomach now. I guess the stress from the day isn't helping. Don't worry, I'll be fine in a minute," she said, her cheeks returning to a pale pink, which he liked a lot better than the ghost-white hue from a few minutes ago.

He stood there another couple of seconds, not wanting to leave her.

"It's already settling down," she said, urging him to go.

Ryder nodded, only because she looked steady on her feet and her lips were pink again.

Inside, he located a bottle of water and a package of saltines next to the dustiest can of Campbell's soup he'd ever seen. At least they had crackers. His mother used to give him 7Up to settle his stomach, so he grabbed a bottle of that, too. As for himself, a shot of black coffee was all he needed to keep his mind clear. He poured a large cup.

Ryder pulled a twenty out of his money clip as he heard what he thought sounded like a muffled scream coming from outside.

A quick glance out the window warned that something was dead wrong. There was an SUV angled toward his pickup, blocking Ryder's view.

He tossed the twenty on the counter and tore out of that store faster than the clerk could say that he forgot his items. Suddenly none of those mattered. Not while Faith might be in trouble.

FAITH TRIED TO scream again, but a hand clamped over her mouth. She'd thought the SUV that had pulled up beside Ryder's truck was there to use the air pump until a man had come around the side toward her. Then it had dawned on her that this was the same SUV that had followed her before.

The man's dark beady eyes that had been focused on her left no room for doubt about his intention—he was coming for her. The rest of his face was covered and she couldn't get a good look at him. She'd bolted. Her weak legs had threatened to give out, and that was the only reason the man caught up to her.

He'd hauled her off her feet and was carting her toward the familiar-looking SUV. She could see that there was another man at the wheel, but his features were hidden behind sunglasses and a bandanna. If the guy holding her managed to get her another twenty yards and inside that truck, there'd be nothing Ryder could do.

She twisted and turned but couldn't shake free from his viselike grip. She had to think fast or he'd stuff her inside the cab and they'd be gone.

Lifting up her right foot, she jabbed it backward with all the strength she could muster, scoring a direct hit with the heel of her boot to his groin.

He grunted and dropped to his knees, taking her down with him. She popped up on all fours, struggling to gain purchase in the gravel. If she could crawl, claw or scoot to Ryder's truck she could hop inside and lock the doors.

"Ryder," she managed to shout through heaves as she scrambled to her feet.

She succeeded in gaining a few steps of forward progress before a hand closed around her ankle, the iron grip brought her down flat on her face. She hit the pavement hard; her hands smacking down first were the only things keeping her head from banging against the cracked surface.

Before she could get her bearings, she was being hauled upright again. The driver was there, too, gripping her around the midsection as Dark Eyes clutched her legs from behind. There was no fighting her way out of this one, but that didn't stop her from trying. She kicked, twisted and screamed. Her only prayer was that the baby wasn't being somehow hurt in the process.

She glanced up and screamed again in time to see that Ryder had heard her and he was already barreling toward her.

He was going to be too late, she thought as she was being tossed inside the cab of the SUV.

"That man coming toward us is Ryder O'Brien. You won't get away with…whatever it is you're planning to do to me. And if you do, that man will see to it that both of you rot in jail or don't live long enough to see another sunrise. So think very hard about your next move." Threatening was the last line of defense, and she could only pray it would work.

The driver shot a look toward Dark Eyes. "Hey, man. I didn't know an O'Brien was involved. That wasn't part of the deal."

"She never told me anything. I don't care who he is. *Go*, or we'll both end up in jail," Dark Eyes demanded.

"Who is *she*?" Faith asked. If the men were talking about being hired by a woman, then her father couldn't be involved. Could he?

Chapter Six

Ryder hopped inside his truck and jabbed his foot onto the gas pedal. The forest green late-model SUV was fifty yards ahead as he navigated onto the road. The license plate had been removed so there was no way to call this in and get Tommy's help. Since this was outside Tommy's area he couldn't do much except make a call to the local sheriff. Not unless the driver took her into Collier County where Tommy had jurisdiction.

Even so, Ryder would see it snow in the middle of a Texas summer before he'd allow these jerks to get away with Faith. They'd better not harm a hair on her head if they knew what was good for them. Or do anything that might hurt the baby growing inside her…

A solid wall of frustration and helplessness slammed into Ryder. He felt a knife cutting through his chest, ripping out his heart.

And that sent all kinds of confusing emotions slashing through him.

He understood his feelings for Faith, no matter how complicated they'd become. Hell, they'd defied logic from day one. But a baby he hadn't even met yet? How could he be ready to trade his own life for a little carpet-crawler he hadn't even seen? Faith barely had a bump as far as he could tell. But that didn't matter to Ryder. All his protective instincts were jacked into high gear and the thought of losing anyone else bit through him, hard and sharp. Residual feelings from losing his parents?

He was making good progress toward the SUV when brake lights surprised him and the vehicle pulled to a complete stop in the middle of the road. Ryder followed the driver's lead, keeping a few yards of distance between them in case they opened fire. Adrenaline shot through the roof. He opened his door and eased out, making sure to keep metal in between him and the SUV in front in case someone started shooting. His pulse hammered and all he could think was how much the men would pay if they did anything to hurt Faith or his child.

He expected to see one of the men and was shocked when Faith stepped out instead. Her hands were high in the air as she turned toward him.

Were the men baiting Ryder? Did they have plans to hurt her? Right in front of his eyes?

He slid his right hand in the back floorboard until he felt his shotgun. If these guys decided to be stupid enough to hurt Faith in any way or send metal his direction, he planned to take them both down. Leave Faith unharmed and they could live. The thought of watching as Faith was shot hit him harder than a physical punch.

Faith started walking toward him. *One step at a time. That's right.* He had no idea what these guys were up to, but he planned to be ready for anything.

"Don't follow us and we won't hurt the lady, okay?" the driver shouted and there was too much tension in his voice.

Could it be that easy? Or was this a trap?

The man was staring at Ryder from behind the barrel of a rifle, and Ryder couldn't get a good description of him.

"You got it, man." Ryder's heart hammered harder against his rib cage. A few more feet and Faith would be home free. He didn't dare make a sudden move for fear the driver would react.

"We don't want trouble," the driver said.

"You get her and we drive away. No police. No trouble. Got it?"

"No one's been hurt so no harm's been done," Ryder said. "That changes and we're talking a different story."

"You're cool with the terms?" The tension in the driver's voice had all the hairs on Ryder's neck pricked.

"As long as nothing happens to the lady, I have no reason to go after you," Ryder shouted back. A few more steps and she'd be close enough for him to make a move to save her if the driver fired. He'd throw himself in front of her to block the path if needed.

"Throw your keys into the field," the driver barked.

Ryder did.

Even so, this was too easy, and Ryder figured that as soon as she got to him the driver and whoever else was in the SUV would open fire. Then the driver surprised him a second time by sliding into the cab and pulling away.

Ryder bolted toward Faith, putting himself between her and the truck as it sped away.

"Are you hurt?" Ryder asked, taking her in his arms and pulling her around the door of his own cab to shield them both.

Her heart pounded against his chest and her body trembled.

"I'm fine," she said, clearly shaken, but her defiant chin shot up, strong. Or maybe she was just too stubborn to let herself show fear. Probably a little of both, having grown up with three older brothers who didn't exactly have a reputation for being soft on anyone.

"They were afraid of you," she said before burying her face in his chest. "That's the only reason they let me walk away."

"How do they know me?" He lifted her chin up so he could examine the scrapes on her face to make sure she didn't need emergency care.

"I told them your name. I said you'd hunt them down and throw them in jail yourself or kill them if they hurt me, and they started panicking," she said, gripping handfuls of his shirt as if holding on for dear life.

"That was smart. You did the right thing," he reassured her, surprising himself by kissing her on the forehead. He tried to convince himself that he'd done it for her and not himself. Her physical scrapes weren't as bad as he'd feared, but he had no idea what taking a fall like she had might do to a baby. Then there was the stress she'd been under. Worrying about Nicholas had been bad enough, but this? "How do you feel?"

"Like I could use a good cup of chamomile

tea," she said on a half sob, half laugh. It was her nervous tic and a good sign.

Still, he wasn't ready to relax yet.

"Think you need to see a doctor?" he asked. "Just to make sure everything's okay."

"I think I'm fine, nothing more than a good scare, but you have a good point. It wouldn't hurt to be on the safe side," she conceded, and he was grateful that she didn't argue. His biggest fear was that she was in shock, and therefore, the pain hadn't kicked in yet. The thought of chasing after the men who did this to her crossed his mind. No way could he risk it with her in the truck. He'd have to let this one go. But he would find them. There was no question about that.

"They said something about a woman giving them this job," she said with emphasis on the word *woman*.

Was she trying to point out that her father couldn't be involved, or convince herself? It was possible that someone had discovered Nicholas was a McCabe, kidnapped him and tried to get a quick ransom out of the senior McCabe. Effort was being made to keep law enforcement out of the picture. A person could've set Nicholas up and tucked the note in the house while Celeste was at work, figuring McCabe would pay and the boy would be home before his mother realized what was going on.

"They can't mean Hannah. This is too complicated for a teenager to coordinate." He'd let ideas churn in the back of his mind while he found a hospital for Faith. This stress couldn't be good for the baby. Ryder helped her into the truck, retrieved his keys and then checked for the nearest ER using the GPS locator on his phone, pausing occasionally to scan the road in order to make sure the men didn't have a change of heart.

He plugged in an address and they arrived fifteen minutes later.

Being inside an ER brought back a flood of bad memories that Ryder wasn't prepared to face. Feelings about walking inside the hospital after learning that his parents had died resurfaced, and his chest tightened. The sound of boots clicking on the tile floors was another reminder. Everything had been drowned out but that sound, as his brothers filed into the room to learn the news, their somber expressions stamped in his thoughts. The news that their parents had been in a fatal car crash hit full force as if Ryder was hearing it again for the first time.

An image of Faith in the same situation rocked him.

Ryder forced his thoughts to the present. This was different. He was here with Faith and she was alive, he reminded himself as she was ushered into a small room. She held on to his arm, her grip a little too tight for him to relax.

"What's your name, honey?" the intake nurse asked after a few routine-sounding questions about what had brought her to the ER today.

A billing clerk stood at the doorway, clipboard in hand.

"Deborah Kerr," Faith said.

Ryder leaned against the wall staring at Faith, wondering why she'd just given them the name of her favorite classic movie star. Then it occurred to him that she'd need to give her insurance card. It took another second for him to realize that she wouldn't want to give out personal information to strangers for fear an ER bill would show up at her door later and alert her family to the fact that she was pregnant.

"I'm responsible for the bill. She lost her insurance when she was laid off from work a couple of months ago," he said, covering for her.

"My name's Kayla. Any unusual pains today, Deborah?" the nurse asked.

"Not right now. Not pain." Faith shot a furtive glance in his direction.

"How about bleeding?" Kayla continued, unaware of the signals being sent between them.

"No. Nothing. Just a little bit of cramping," Faith said. Didn't that kick Ryder's heart rate up.

"You mentioned that you'll be financially responsible?" the nurse asked Ryder.

"Yes," he agreed. "I'm the father of Ms. Kerr's child."

Faith's cheeks flamed bright red.

The nurse nodded, shooting him a look like she understood their situation was complicated. That was a great word to describe everything that had to do with Faith, Ryder thought. And especially covered all the emotions he had roaring through him right now—a mix of confusion and stress and overprotective instincts.

"The billing clerk will finish processing the paperwork at her station," the nurse said to Ryder. "Do you mind following her?"

"Not at all," he said, but that wasn't entirely true. He didn't want to leave Faith's side.

Another quick glance from her said it was okay to leave her alone. She wasn't exactly by herself. She had the nurse.

By the time he came back fifteen minutes later, Faith had on a hospital gown and had her eyes closed with her head resting against a pillow. He slipped inside the room, trying not to disturb her.

"Hi," she said, opening her eyes and glancing at the IV sticking out of her arm.

"Hey there," Ryder said, tamping down the stress at seeing her in a hospital bed.

"They want me to get started on IV fluids since I've been vomiting so much. I may have let myself get a little dehydrated," she said in a voice so soft that Ryder sat on the edge of the bed to get close enough to hear. "I'm sure it's just nerves with Nicholas missing and everything that's happened since."

He nodded. This wasn't the time for the conversation he wanted to have about her letting him take the lead on finding Nicholas. She needed to strap herself in bed and stay there until the baby was born as far as Ryder was concerned.

"The nurse seemed a little too eager to get me out of the room earlier," he said.

Faith smiled. "You should've heard the questions she asked once you left."

"Like what?"

"She wanted to know if I was being abused." She laughed, but it wasn't funny to Ryder.

"That's nice of her," he said defensively.

"She was just doing her job. She didn't mean anything personally by it," she said. "The statistics are staggering. She rattled off a few when I had the same reaction as you. A woman is beaten every nine seconds in America."

Ryder clenched his hands, making tight fists.

"She obviously doesn't know your family or its reputation, or she wouldn't have had to ask," Faith said, clearly picking up on his disgust. A look passed behind her honey browns that he couldn't easily read, another sign things had changed since they'd been together.

"Abuse happens in wealthy families as often as it does in poor." *Every woman should be safe with the person she loved*, he thought bitterly. "I'm more concerned about you than my reputation right now. Feeling any better?"

"I'm probably going to have a few bruises on my face. I saw the red marks when I asked to go to the bathroom before the nurse put the IV in. That'll be fun to explain to my family."

He started to speak his mind, but thought better of it. Again, this wasn't the time to bring up her relationship with her family or why he thought she needed to come clean with them about the pregnancy and her relationship to him. The sooner they all knew that he planned to be part of the baby's life the faster they could all adjust to the fact that they were tied together by that little boy or girl she was carrying.

"It's more important for you to rest and take care of yourself right now," he said, thinking of how much more protective he'd be of a little one once he held the baby in his arms.

"I didn't plan on this." Her hand rested on her tummy. "Now that it's here I don't want to lose it even though that makes no sense. Is that crazy?"

"No." He shared the sentiment. It would take some time to get used to the idea that he was going to be a father. He had four months to adjust. Ryder wasn't sure if that was enough time or not since he'd never been in this situation before, not even a scare because he was always careful, but he'd do whatever it took. For now, he needed to make sure she was safe. "You didn't recognize those men."

She shook her head. "I still can't believe they let me go. I threatened them using your name and they said *she* didn't mention anything about an O'Brien being involved."

Maybe one of McCabe's exes thought she could get his attention by kidnapping his son.

His mind circled back to greed being behind this.

The doctor came in, interrupting them. She was younger than Ryder had expected, and part of him hoped she wasn't too green. He suppressed the urge to ask her age.

She introduced herself as Dr. Field and shook Ryder's outstretched hand. She moved to the bed beside Faith and asked a few routine-sounding questions. A bad feeling settled over Ryder. It could be Faith's revelation. Being in a hospital also brought back too many haunting memories of waiting on word of his parents.

"Have you had any bleeding since the fall?" Dr. Field asked Faith as Ryder, once again, stood helplessly by.

Faith said the same thing she'd told the nurse about the cramping.

He didn't figure there was any way he'd be able to talk Faith into seeing Dr. McConnell later given that the doctor knew everyone in town. He trusted McConnell, since she was a close friend of his mother's. He could see how Faith wouldn't feel as secure.

Ryder had to figure out a way to gently break the news to his brothers that Faith McCabe was having his child. This news would come out of the blue for them. He'd never once mentioned dating anyone, and they'd never suspect he'd see a McCabe. That one wasn't going to go over very well. They, just like her family, would have to get used to it. He knew that his would support him no matter what. But Faith's? Hers was dysfunctional. There were no indications of physical abuse, but mental abuse was just as bad and left no outward signs. He thought about abuse statistics and her mother. She'd been married to Hollister McCabe for a few decades. What would that do to a person?

Ryder would find a way to shield his child. This situation wasn't going away, and since the thought of losing the baby left a weird pain in his chest, he didn't want it to. Not that he would've picked this timing to have a child. Clearly, he'd had no plans before this surprise. He needed to get his head around how his life was about to change.

Four months.

Ryder could figure anything out in sixteen weeks.

"I don't see any reason why you can't go home once that bag is empty," the doctor said, pointing to the pole by her bed. How old was she? Twenty-two? Her credibility wasn't helped by the fact that she wore adult braces.

Faith tensed on the word *home*.

"Thank you," she said.

"I'll send someone in to check you out in a few minutes," Dr. Field said.

Out of courtesy, Ryder thanked the doctor before she left. It sure wasn't because he thought she knew what she was doing.

"You should see a real doctor when we get back to Bluff," he said in a low voice once he was sure the door was closed.

"What was she, like, sixteen?" Faith asked, a smile breaking out over white teeth.

"I wanted to ask what her SAT scores were and what she planned to do after high school graduation," he quipped, grateful for the break in tension. A lighter mood was welcome at this point. It had been one hell of a day, and his normally cool emotions were all over the map, not to mention the chemistry between them hadn't dimmed despite their circumstances.

The rest of the time spent while waiting for the IV bag to drain went by fast. Checkout was speedy and the two were back on the road soon after.

Ryder had a lot on his mind, and the deeper they dug into Nicholas's disappearance, the more questions mounted. The two men who'd tried to abduct Faith were obviously hired by someone. Who? And again, why? He had to wonder what these men, and Hannah, could want from a fifteen-year-old boy. Ransom was the only thing that made sense, and he doubted that Hollister McCabe would pay anything for an illegitimate child. But then whoever took him might not know that.

"Where do we go now?" Faith asked.

"You? Home." There was going to be no argument over that one.

"I can't. Nicholas is still missing."

"Did you get a good look at the kidnappers? Can you describe them?"

"We can't go to police," she insisted. "They might hurt him."

"They didn't seem like the most skilled criminals or even like they'd thought their plan completely through when they snatched you," he said, eyes on the road ahead. "I keep going back to the same question. What do they stand to gain from taking Nicholas, and my mind keeps cycling back to the same response…money."

"Me, too. I mean, those guys were scary as all get-out and strong. But they hear your name and are willing to let me go. I'm grateful, believe me, but I can't figure what that's all about," she said.

"It makes more sense now that I know there's someone else pulling the strings,"

Ryder said. "Those guys were only willing to go so far."

"Maybe they were just trying to scare me in order to stop me from investigating Nicholas's disappearance," she offered.

"That's possible," he said. "So, whoever's doing this doesn't know you very well."

"Then they most likely planned to release me all along. So I wasn't in as much danger as I—"

"Hold it right there," Ryder interrupted. "I see exactly where you're going with this and there's no way I'm standing by and watching you—"

"That's why I came to you," she said.

"We need to involve the law. I understand that you want to put Nicholas first—"

"Because he's in danger. I would do the same thing for this baby. Besides, Celeste is going to the sheriff to report Nicholas missing." Ryder wouldn't get far as long as her defenses were up.

"I get it. I do," he soothed, figuring he needed to take another tack. "Today has been a long day. You've barely been able to keep food down and the only reason you're hydrated is because you just spent an hour on an IV. If you're not ready to go home you can rest at the cabin. I'll keep working on finding Nicholas. You don't have to do this alone now, and I won't stop until I have answers. You have my word on that."

"Okay," Faith said, and his chest swelled with pride that his word meant something to her. "Take me to the cabin. I can't go home right now."

FAITH WOKE WITH a start. She sat up and glanced around, trying to get her bearings. The last thing she remembered was curling up on the couch at the cabin.

The clock on the mantel read eight forty-five. It was dark outside. Her mouth was dry. And she needed to go to the bathroom. Another great pregnancy side effect was an almost constant need to use the restroom.

Her stomach cramped as she pushed off the oversize tan suede sofa. That had happened a lot in her first trimester and she'd called her doctor to make sure everything was okay. Into her second trimester, it'd stopped and she gave in to a moment of fear that something was wrong with the baby.

She checked outside and Ryder's truck was gone. Only her car was still there.

Keeping a positive attitude had gotten her through many dark days, and so she chose to think positively now, too. And that lasted right up until she saw the blood. There wasn't much. But it was enough to get her heart racing and cause fear to threaten to swallow her.

She needed to call Ryder and find out where he was.

By the time Faith made it back to the couch, she'd calmed herself down. Spotting was completely normal, and the cramp was gone. That had to be a good sign.

Instead of involving Ryder, she phoned her doctor's private line.

He picked up on the second ring.

She explained what had happened and he reassured her, as he had so many times in the first trimester, that it was most likely nothing. If it worsened, she was to go directly to the hospital. She thanked the doctor, grateful for the reassurance.

Despite being stressed, she was hungry. She moved into the kitchen. There was a note on the fridge from Ryder. *Food's in the fridge. Help yourself. I'll be back later.*

She found a few of her favorite things, including fresh red apples and Greek yogurt. There was a box of graham crackers on the counter and a container of decaf coffee.

Thinking about how many times he'd "fixed" her breakfast—which basically meant half-burned toast, yogurt and fruit with a good cup of coffee—had her heart doing things she couldn't afford. She would always be a McCabe. He would always be an O'Brien. And there wasn't a bridge long enough to cover that gap.

It was getting late. Spending so much time with Ryder today had taken a toll. Every time he was close, her body was aware of his all-male presence. And since her increased hormone levels amplified all her senses, she felt even more attracted to him.

The sexual chemistry pinging between them could almost drive her to distraction. And her stubborn heart tried to tell her that her feelings for him had grown. It was probably for the best that he wasn't at the cabin. She'd driven her car to meet Ryder at the cabin early this morning, so she didn't have to wait for him to get a ride. She needed to get home to check on her mother. There were other things she needed to investigate at home, too, like her father's private study.

Chapter Seven

Faith slipped inside the back door at the ranch and took the rear staircase up to her room, thinking her life would've been far less complicated if she'd moved to the city after college instead of coming home to learn the family business and look after her mother—a mother who had her increasingly worried lately.

She went straight to her en suite bathroom and stripped off her clothes. Stepping into the shower, she felt the warm water sluicing over her sore body. She took her time washing off, giving herself permission not to think about her missing brother for a few minutes. *Or Ryder*, a little voice added.

She looked down at her growing stomach as she toweled off. Her pants no longer fit, and it wouldn't be long before her belly would be too big to cover and she'd have no choice but to tell her parents. A clean oversize T-shirt and pajama pants hid her small bump. *Not for long, little bean.*

Thankfully, there hadn't been any more spotting since earlier in the evening.

A quick mirror check, a little face powder and her scrapes and bruises were concealed fairly well. She'd left the door between her bedroom and bathroom cracked open and she cradled her stomach with one hand as she walked into her bedroom.

Her mother sat on the edge of her bed in the dark. Faith jumped and let out a little yelp.

"Sorry, sweetheart. I didn't mean to scare you," her mother said, sounding distant. That wasn't a good sign.

Faith's blood pressure hit triple time. *Breathe.*

"Everything okay, Mom?" she asked, dropping her hand to her side and praying that her mother hadn't noticed. Faith needed to find Nicholas and put the next phase of her plan into action—a plan that was far more complicated now that Ryder knew the truth.

"You didn't come home. I was worried," Mom said, embracing her in a tight hug. Her hands were so cold.

"I was out with friends." It wasn't exactly a lie. Although her heart would argue that she and Ryder had been so much more.

Mom's shoulders deflated.

"Have you seen your father?" Her mother stared at the wall.

"Not today. Why?" Faith turned on the soft light on her nightstand and then moved closer to her mother, dropping down by her side.

Her eyes carried dark circles as she sat there wringing her hands together.

"He's not home. Didn't make it to supper, either," she said, and she sounded on the verge of tears. With her mother so involved in her own situation Faith figured she was too distraught to notice any physical changes in her and was grateful.

Faith rubbed her mother's back. "It's okay. He'll be home. He's probably out with a business partner. You know, making another deal."

"Or maybe he's with that woman again," her mother said, sounding a little hysterical.

Faith stopped herself from asking which one.

"I'm sure he's just tied up with work, as usual." Faith hated lying. "I'll be dealing with the paperwork from his deals until the end of summer."

Her mother just sat there, her gaze fixed on a spot on the opposite wall.

"Come on. Let's get you ready for bed," Faith said, urging her mother to her feet. She was probably off her medication again. Faith would get an anxiety pill and tuck her mother into bed.

Her mother mumbled a few words that Faith didn't quite catch as she helped her into her pajamas.

"Stay right here, okay?" Faith asked, helping her to the massive four-poster bed she shared with Faith's father. The bed looked so grand and so…empty. Sadness fell like a curtain as she thought about how lonely her mother's life must be. And here, Faith was about to make it worse. She could only hope that her mother would be okay. Guilt assaulted her again at the thought of leaving her mother alone in a mentally abusive relationship.

The woman still looked distraught, and Faith wasn't sure if she could trust her mother to stay put. In her heightened emotional state, the last thing she needed to do was wander the house by herself. Anything could happen. Faith had found her mother curled up in a ball in a corner of the dining room, shaking, with only a light gown on in the dead of winter once. Faith had just turned twelve. There were other times, too. Once her mother had taken too much medication and wandered into the backyard. She'd fallen into the pool and if Faith's golden retriever, Sparks, hadn't barked, her mother would've drowned. She'd been too out of it to realize she was about to die.

Her mother's emotions had been overwrought lately, and she was a walking ball of nerves.

Shaking off the bad memories, Faith retrieved the bottle of little white pills from her mother's medicine cabinet and a glass of water from the sink.

"Here you go. Take this and he'll be home before you open your eyes," Faith soothed. How many times had she gone through this routine with her mother in the past year? Things were escalating, and Faith could only pray her mother would take the step and get help someday. Guilt hit her again at the thought of leaving the woman behind.

"He's coming home?" her mother asked, calmer after the medicine starting kicking in.

"That's right. He's on his way. All you have to do is close your eyes and when you open them again he'll be right next to you," Faith said. She sat with her mother until she fell asleep, thinking about how vibrant she'd been when Faith was young.

The thought of walking away, leaving her permanently, didn't sit well with Faith, but she would have no choice. How much longer could she get away with no one noticing her bump? Or realizing that she hadn't worn a pair of jeans in weeks even though it was cold outside? She'd barely managed to get through those first few months of feeling like she wanted to barf all the time without raising any red flags.

Luckily, her father worked outside most of the day and spent most of his evenings with "business partners." He had a huge office in the barn. He'd said it was to be close to his men so he could keep an eye on his workers.

Inside the house, he maintained a private study, and that door was almost always locked.

Faith glanced down at her mother. Hollister McCabe's love was toxic. Her eyes were closed and her breathing had changed to a steady rhythm. Faith tiptoed out of the room. She could've stomped and her mother wouldn't know the difference. And that broke Faith's heart.

Instead of going to her own room, she checked out front for her father's Suburban. It was gone. Rather than head back upstairs, she hooked a right and walked to the back of the house, to her father's study. She picked up the spare key that had been tucked inside the vase in the hall bath and unlocked the door.

If she'd thought, she would've brought her

phone with her and turned on the flashlight app. As it was, she'd have to rely on the dim light from the hallway in case her father returned. The ranch was huge, and she wouldn't be able to hear him pull in. The wood paneling made the room even darker. Doubt crept in.

This was crazy. She couldn't see anything. She heard a noise in the hallway and her heart skipped a beat.

Her father wasn't home, she reminded herself. Her mother was asleep. The hired workers at the McCabe ranch all slept in separate bunks in the barns. Women who worked inside shared adjoining rooms in the horse barn. There was a foreman and several hired hands who slept in the second barn. Her brothers were almost never home this early. There shouldn't be anyone in the house but Faith and her mother. Their interaction left Faith unsettled and that's the reason she was jumpy.

Time was running out and she needed to make her move soon. All she needed was to find Nicholas. Then she could disappear.

She made sure to keep all the lights off in case someone came home. She had three brothers who would be quick to bust her if they found her in their dad's private study.

Her father's desk had a couple of stacks of

paperwork on top. She fanned through the first stack, determined not to upset the documents. Most of those were bills and a few others were contracts marked with a Post-it note for his signature. There was nothing earth-shattering there. Although she had no idea what she was looking for. Even though she'd denied Ryder's accusations that her father could somehow be behind Nicholas's disappearance, he'd planted a seed in her mind that had taken root and she needed to know that her father wasn't somehow involved.

The possibility that Celeste could be the female involved died quickly. Celeste had taken care of Nicholas on her own with little money for fifteen years. She wouldn't use him to get back at Faith's father.

A noise sounded in the hallway and Faith froze. She hadn't heard her father's Suburban. Was there any possibility that her mother could be walking around?

She stood for a quiet moment until she was sure the coast was clear. She touched her belly, thinking how she would never put her own child through any of this mess.

The built-in set of drawers on the right-hand side of his desk held tax documents and titles of ownership for various pieces of property and equipment. The large drawer on the left had a few boxes of keepsakes, one from her grandfather. The middle drawer was locked. Faith felt around for a key but didn't find one. No, her father wouldn't be careless enough to keep a key so close. *Especially not if he has something inside that drawer that he doesn't want people to find*, a voice in the back of her mind said. She dismissed it as letting Ryder influence her too much.

She pulled out a hairpin and played around with the lock, listening for the *snick* that said she'd hit the right spot to release the mechanism. Living with three brothers had taught her to be resourceful, especially when it came to getting inside their rooms when she needed something. All three boys locked their doors, and part of her had wondered why all the secrecy. So many secrets.

The sound she was waiting for came and with it a jolt of pride for still being able to get the job done as needed. The temporary feeling was replaced with guilt. Was she stooping to her father's level of distrust? Becoming just like him and the boys?

She shuddered at the thought.

Faith rejected the notion that she was anything like her father and the three McCabe brothers. She was like her half brother Nicholas, and she would go to any length to find him even if it meant violating her father's sacred space.

Faith took in a breath and opened the drawer. On top was a legal document. She scanned the page to figure out what it was. A lawsuit? She used her finger to guide her way down the middle of the page looking for the complaint.

There it was in bold letters. He was being sued for paternity, but it wasn't Celeste being named as the complainant. Faith didn't even recognize this woman's name, but apparently her father might have another son. The boy was three years old and the complaint was filed a year ago. Faith was certain that her father's lawyer would get him out of this one just as sure as he'd gotten out of paying Nicholas's mother.

A heavy feeling settled on Faith's chest. Did her mother know about any of these children? She must.

The complainant was a waitress in a café in Louisiana, according to the paperwork. He traveled all over the South and Southwest. Did he leave a string of children and desperate mothers behind? One desperate enough to come after one of his children for revenge?

Faith didn't want to acknowledge this side of her father, this smooth-talking jerk who used women. And yet the documents were staring her in the face, quashing those moments in her childhood when she'd looked up to him for being a smart businessman and a doting father.

She touched her stomach again as a few tears rolled down her cheeks. Her child would never know this kind of pain. The hormones had her ready to cry at a TV commercial if it pulled the right heartstrings, and something about this whole scenario had her missing Ryder. There was something about his presence that made her feel wanted, safe.

Shuffling through the folders inside the drawer mostly made her sad. Sad that this family wasn't enough for her father. Sad for the kids who would grow up without support, alone. Sad for the mothers who'd have to work extra hours. She wiped away the tears and refocused. Was there anything in here about Nicholas?

Rechecking the folders, she caught a piece of paper sticking out from in between two manila folders near the top of the small stack.

Her finger dragged across the name Nicholas Bowden. There it was in plain sight. A report about Nicholas. His whereabouts. His hangouts. There were photos, too.

Faith's heart dropped and her pulse raced.

Because there were pictures of the two of them together.

"Find what you're looking for, Faith?" her father's voice boomed from the doorway.

There was no point in trying to lie her way out of this one.

"How many are there, Father?" She picked up the small stack of files. He'd know full well what she was talking about. "Half a dozen? More?"

"Nothing in my private study is of concern to you," her father said, flipping on the light.

"Everything about this family is just as much my business as it is yours." She held the stack toward him. She tried to use sheer willpower to stop her hands from shaking, but it was no use. "Why don't we wake up Mom and see if she shares your opinion?"

The fire in her father's eyes nearly knocked her back a step.

"You leave your mother out of this or I'll see to it that you never see her again," he fired back. The anger in his voice sent an icy chill down her spine. He meant every word of that threat. Little did he know she was about to disappear on her own.

She'd known her father was dishonest and that he cheated on her mother, but she had no idea the extent of the damage. Part of her didn't want to know, either. Had she put her head in the sand in order to avoid the humiliation?

Yes. Guilt nipped at her.

"Where's Nicholas?" She stood her ground even though everything inside her was screaming to run, to get out of there or hide.

"Leave it alone, Faith."

"I can't. He's innocent and he's a good kid," she kept pushing.

"He's someone else's bastard and he'll never be a McCabe." His angry words were like hot pokers searing her. The little balloon of hope that her father was a better man than this popped, leaving pieces of her heart scattered on the floor.

"Well, then maybe he'll have a chance at a decent life if you have your goons let him go." She threw the accusation out there again to see if it would stick. Her father hadn't exactly denied knowing about Nicholas's disappearance.

"I already told you to stay out of this. What happens to that boy doesn't concern you," he said again, which wasn't a denial of his involvement.

"Is he hurt?" she was shouting now. She stomped across the room and got in her father's face. "What did you do to him?"

"Me?" His brows knit in confusion. "I didn't *do* anything to the boy, and I won't tolerate being blackmailed, either." Fiery darts shot from his glare.

"If you didn't do it, then who?" she managed to say through her blinding anger. The word *blackmail* registered somewhere in the back of her mind.

"I want nothing to do with that boy," he said bitterly. "And I don't have the first idea who's behind all this. I don't care, either. But know this—I don't give a hoot what they do to the child."

"There will be consequences to your actions," she said as she stomped past him. He caught her by the arm.

"Like what? Are you threatening me, little girl?" he said as he squeezed.

"I'm not your little girl," she said, trying to jerk free from his grasp and failing.

"You won't be if you keep messing with that bastard," he ground out. For a split second, she thought he was talking about Ryder. And then she remembered that her father had no problem calling his own son by the derogatory term.

"You're hurting me." She looked into her father's eyes, searching for something. Compassion…love…regret. Anything from the man she used to look up to as a child, used to love. His steel eyes were cold. There was nothing soft or kind left of the man who'd bounced her on his knee.

"No bastard children will ever be recognized as a McCabe." The words were like bullets being fired at her.

She jerked her arm free and pushed past her father. "Is that right? Well, know this. I'm going to find him and do whatever I can to help. And you better not get in my way."

"Leave it alone," he threatened, shouting after her. "Or you're the one who'll deal with consequences."

Her father shouted curses and threats as she made her way back to her room, threw on some clothing, grabbed her purse and keys and then shot out the door.

Tears flooded her eyes as she slid behind the driver's seat and buckled up. She had no doubt that he'd deliver on his threats if she didn't walk away from Nicholas. And she'd never been more certain that he'd turn his back on her the second he found out about the baby she was carrying.

A few deep breaths calmed her enough to stop crying. One more gave her the boost she needed to start her car and drive away. She needed to get as far away from the ranch and her father as possible. Nicholas had been taken for ransom that her father had refused to pay. Fear gripped her. She couldn't allow herself to think that she was too late to save her brother.

The minute she found Nicholas—and she would find him—she needed to get him and her baby out of town and far away. All three of them could start fresh in the quaint house in Michigan that she'd purchased using a dummy company that she'd set up out of her Cayman bank account.

The paperwork to change her last name to her mother's maiden name was almost finalized. Faith had planned this new life for her and her baby, and now she would include Nicholas.

The first phase of her plan was in place.

At this point, she would welcome being kicked out of the family. *What family?* she asked herself through blinding tears. What kind of family treated each other like this? There was no love, just expectations and heartache.

The thought of leaving her mother alone to fend for herself ate at Faith. If she was going to be allowed to stay in contact with her mother, she could never allow the true paternity of her baby to be known. If she had to plead with Ryder to keep her secret, she would.

Faith still hadn't figured out how she was going to handle the situation with Ryder. Part of her, the part that had known she had to tell him all along, was relieved that her secret was out in the open with him. Ryder was a good man and he deserved to know. That fact had warred with the reality that she lived in. The one in which her father's realization would be harmful and toxic to everyone involved.

Could she tell Ryder about her Michigan plan? She wiped away a tear that rolled down her cheek. Maybe they could figure out a way for him to visit the baby without the entire town knowing their business. She held on to that hope as she pulled down the gravel lane.

The fishing cabin was blacked out. Her heart sank at the realization there was no sign of Ryder's truck. It was probably for the best since she didn't need another emotional complication, even if part of her brain argued that being with him was so much better than being without him. Faith parked near the front door. Her headlights would time out automatically in sixty seconds, so she made a mad dash for the cabin.

Exhaustion started wearing on her as she crossed the threshold, closing and locking the door behind her. Pregnancy exacerbated everything. Her need for Ryder felt a thousand times stronger because of her hormones.

And then there was the issue of not getting enough good-quality sleep lately. Her mind was spent, her bones tired. So she let herself think about Ryder and how amazing she'd felt in this very spot not so long ago with his arms curled around her, their legs in a tangle. And the feel of his warm breath against her neck as he feathered kisses there.

RYDER STARED AT the ceiling. It was two o'clock in the morning and he hadn't had any shut-eye. Activities at the ranch would pick up in a few short hours. All he could think about was Faith and if she was okay. She'd disappeared without leaving a note. He'd texted her and she responded with one word. *Home.*

And tonight, the thing that was on his mind the most as he lay in bed unable to sleep was how much he missed being with her, holding her, feeling like she belonged with him—*to him*, a rebellious part of his brain interjected.

Her soft skin, the way her body molded to his…

He threw off the covers and pulled on his jeans, needing to get out and clear his head.

Standing on his back porch, looking up at

the open sky he loved so much, brought no peace tonight. The fact that Ryder was going to be a father hit hard, but not for the reasons he'd suspected. He'd thought there'd be regret—not normally something in his vocabulary—and was surprised when there wasn't a hint of it. He'd need to make a lot of adjustments in his life to be ready for a little one, but the idea itself was starting to take hold. The thing that bothered him was that he'd never have the chance to introduce his child to his parents.

Getting through the holidays without them had been brutal, even for a tough bunch like the O'Briens. Hitting a major milestone like this—becoming a father—and realizing they wouldn't be around for any of it had him gripping the wood railing overlooking his yard so hard his knuckles were white. Texas, this land, was a piece of his soul. And yet even the land he loved couldn't settle his anguish or lessen his pain.

Being here at the ranch without them was hard. Reminders of the two of them were everywhere, even on the porch his mother had insisted on helping decorate. Her touches could be seen in the Kyra Jenkins wildlife bronze sculpture behind his coffee-colored sofa and the matching hand towels in his guest bath. He should've reined her in on that last one, but she'd been beside herself when she'd brought them over. She'd done a good job and his house was cozy. Someday, all of those reminders of her might bring comfort. Now they just made him feel hollowed out.

There was a different feeling settling in his chest since Faith had returned. He was more at ease and yet he couldn't sort out the reason. Not much had changed. His parents' killer hadn't been brought to justice. And yet the hole in his chest was less cavernous. Did that have to do with learning he was going to be a father? Ryder had thought about telling his brothers about the baby Faith was carrying and decided against it. He wasn't ready to talk about it with them, not until he and the mother of his child sorted out important details like how they were going to handle the news with her family. Complicated didn't begin to cover the journey they were about to be on. Speaking of Faith, the thought of her being at the McCabe ranch sat like scalding coffee on his tongue.

It was the middle of the night. He should be tired. Instead, his mind raced. There was no way he was going to be able to go back to sleep now. He didn't want to be on the ranch tonight.

Within five minutes he was on the road, and twenty minutes after that he was pulling up at the fishing cabin.

Faith's car was parked out front and relief flooded him. Ryder stomped the brake. He should turn around and go back home. It was late and his mind played tricks on him, tricks that had him thinking that he wanted to feel her in his arms again, to find that same comfort he'd found there after learning about his parents.

All the lights were out, so he figured she was asleep. He should give her the cabin.

On second thought, someone had tried to kidnap her earlier. It might have been a scare tactic, as she wanted to believe. She'd said the guys who'd taken her didn't want to get on the wrong side of the O'Brien family. So those guys wouldn't likely make a second attempt. Didn't exactly mean she was safe. Whoever sent them could've hired someone else to finish the job by now. Then there was the issue of her father. Ryder didn't trust Hollister McCabe. And he couldn't shake the feeling that the man was somehow involved in Nicholas's disappearance.

Instead of making a U-turn, Ryder pulled into the spot next to hers and parked.

Protecting his child was the reason Ryder told himself that he'd parked his truck and was heading inside. And not because he needed to see Faith.

Chapter Eight

Ryder closed the bedroom door and then made a pot of coffee using the light on the vent hood in order to see in the small kitchen. Knowing that Faith was sleeping in the next room played havoc with his pulse but was so much better than before when she'd left without a note. She still had that effect on him, the one that had him wanting to touch her soft skin and get lost in her fresh-after-a-spring-rain flowers-and-sunshine scent.

How many times had they slept twisted in the sheets with their bodies fused together in that very room? Exhaustion from making love sometimes two or three times in a row having zapped their energy and forced them to finally give in to sleep.

The memories were burned into his brain not just because the sex was mind-blowing—it was. Sex couldn't be this good with anyone else because he felt a connection to Faith that he'd never experienced with another woman. Sex was sex. The physical act was always good. No woman before Faith had ever fit his body the way she had. He'd never felt as content afterward with anyone else, either. And that had a lot to do with what happened in between rounds. Faith was easy to talk to. She was smart and had a quirky sense of humor. It didn't hurt that she was beautiful. She was just as attractive when she was fresh from the shower and her hair was pulled back in a loose ponytail, maybe even more so, than when she was all done up.

Thinking about their past and the times they'd spent together under this very roof stirred areas that didn't need to be awake at this hour and especially without the prospect of release. His body was keenly aware of her being in the next room.

Ryder took a sip of black coffee, hoping it would clear his thoughts and steer him away from the dangerous territory he was dipping into. It was the past, and best left far behind. They had a new reality to deal with. Five days of Nicholas missing.

The door to the bedroom opened and Faith stood there, wearing only one of his old T-shirts like she'd done countless times. His heart stirred at the same time blood flew south, awakening areas he'd have to work to ignore.

"I hope it's okay that I came back here," she said. Her voice had that low sleepy quality that was enough to tip him over the edge and make him want things he shouldn't. Another thing he couldn't afford to notice right now, since his better judgment had hit the trail, was how sexy her hair was when it was tousled and loose around her shoulders. Or how long and silky her legs were.

"I'm glad you did." Ryder took another sip of hot coffee, focusing on the warm burn on his throat. Holding his mug kept his fingers busy. And that was good because they wanted to do things that would get him into more trouble, like tangle in her hair and haul her body against his.

"You were right about my father," she said, taking a few tentative steps toward him. Her voice cracked like she was on the verge of tears.

And that was enough to dampen any sexual thoughts he'd been having. It was just as well. He forced his gaze away from the V that fell over her full breasts, exposing just enough skin for him to be able to remember planting kisses along that trail a few short months ago.

Her breathing was erratic, and he felt electricity ping between them as she joined him in the small kitchen despite the fact that she was about to cry.

"You want a cup of coffee?" he asked, tamping down his own inappropriate thoughts.

"No, thanks. I can't." Her hand went to her stomach.

Right. He hadn't really thought about how much she'd already had to sacrifice for the pregnancy. How much more she'd be sacrificing when she had the baby. Her father would disown her for sleeping with an O'Brien. He'd cut her off financially in a heartbeat.

Not a problem, Ryder thought. He had enough money to take care of her and their child. It was just as much his doing as it was hers that she was in this situation, and no child of his would want for any necessities.

She stepped past him and his nose filled with her scent as she pulled a glass out of the cupboard. Ryder tried not to notice her sweet bottom or the silky-smooth skin of her thighs when the T-shirt rode up.

He forced himself to look in the other direction. It took considerable effort. She filled the glass with water from the sink and turned around to face him.

The two were in close proximity because the kitchen was built for one.

"Did you find something in his office?" he asked, needing to redirect his thoughts.

"He knows about Nicholas's disappearance, won't pay ransom, and I have no idea how I'm going to find my brother now. We had a confrontation," she said. "He doesn't care about my brother."

Talking about Hollister McCabe was sobering enough to quell any sexual thoughts Ryder had been having.

"Tell me what happened," he said, motioning toward the couch.

She shook her head, pacing in the small area between the kitchen and the living room instead.

"He caught me in his office and we exchanged a few heated words," she said. "I can't go home again."

"What makes you think you can't go back?" Ryder was relieved because he didn't want her there.

"He threatened me." Her gaze dropped down to her stomach and bounced up again. "It's no longer safe for me or the baby."

His grip tightened on the handle of his coffee mug and he clenched his jaw. At least she had that part right. Ryder didn't want his child anywhere near Hollister McCabe. "What did he say about Nicholas?"

"That he had no plans to give in to blackmail. He called Nicholas a bastard." She paced faster. "Can you believe that?"

Sadly, he could. That, and so much more about the senior McCabe. He wondered how Faith had turned out so normal given the family she'd grown up in. Her three brothers were trouble, and her mother seemed like a fragile woman the few times he'd seen her in town.

"I'm sorry." He could tell that she loved Nicholas and he knew how much her father's rejection would hurt her.

"I mean, can you even imagine?" she asked, her voice rising in anger. "It's his own son and yet he called him a bastard. And Nicholas is the only good brother I have."

Becoming upset wouldn't be good for her or the baby. Ryder needed to figure out a way to calm her down…

Nothing immediately came to mind, since he'd never been much of a talker. So he pulled her into his arms.

"I know," he said, trying to soothe the frustration making her heart beat so rapidly against his chest. The man needed to be in jail, and yet he couldn't voice his opinion out loud. He could already see that it was hard enough for her to realize that her father wasn't the man she'd hoped he was.

Faith leaned into him and she looked up into his eyes. He sensed the second her body became aware of being fused with his.

Ryder should let go and back away slowly, because this situation was a powder keg. Logic flew out the window with common sense as she pressed harder against him. The feel of her full breasts against his chest spiked his blood pressure in an all too familiar way. He let his hands drop to her waist and then encircled her with his arms. No matter what else he felt toward her, Faith was a beautiful woman. Even more so now.

Her hands came up, palms flat against his chest. He wasn't sure if she was going to push him away, but his answer came in the form of her fists closing around his shirt and tugging him toward her. He was already hard and his erection strained against the zipper of his jeans as he breathed in her fresh-April-shower scent, all flowers and warmth.

He should probably stop himself before this went too far, or ask her if she thought this was really a good idea. He didn't do either. Instead, he dipped his head down and pressed his mouth against hers—something he'd been wanting to do far too long and had been denied. Her lips were soft against his, molding to his.

She raised her hands, tunneling her fingers into his hair. He brought his up, his fingers curling around the base of her neck, positioning her so he could really kiss her. In the space of one deep breath, her lips parted and his tongue slid inside her mouth. The taste of her, honey and mint, crashed down around him as memory merged with the here and now. How long had he been needing to do this?

Too long.

And that damn question resurfaced as to whether or not this was a good idea. Ryder had to force restraint, so he put a little physical space in between them first. That he could do easily because he didn't want to do anything that might hurt the baby growing in her stomach. Primal urge had him wanting to rip off her T-shirt and panties, lift her onto the counter, and drive his pulsing erection deep inside her. Her hands were all over him, roaming his arms and back. She was driving him insane with need.

But would it somehow hurt the baby?

With all the effort he could muster, he pulled back.

"Faith—"

"Don't say it," she said breathlessly.

"You don't think this is a question we need to ask ourselves before...?"

"No. I don't." Faith crossed her arms, grabbed the hem of the T-shirt she wore and pulled it over her head. She let it go and it tumbled to the kitchen floor. Next, she shimmied out of her pale blue panties, and that nearly did Ryder in. She stood there, arms at her sides. There was enough light for him to see every curve of her body clearly. Her breasts were fuller than before, her hips a little more round, and he suspected that the changes had to do with the pregnancy. Her body had been beautiful before but he found her even sexier with a few more curves.

She was close enough for him to see her pulse pound wildly at the base of her throat. His groin strained as he took in her form. His gaze slid down her body, pausing at the small strip of hair at her mound.

"Don't just look at me. I'm right here. I want you to touch me, Ryder." She took a step toward him, cutting the space between them in half. Her delicate skin was flushed with desire and her honey-brown eyes glittered with need.

"You know I won't be able to hold back if you take one more step toward me," he warned, and it was more for him than her. Of course, he would stop at any point if she told him to or gave him a sign that she wasn't absolutely certain this was a good idea.

"Give me one good reason we shouldn't do this," she said, that defiance he loved about her twinkling in her eyes.

"The baby," he said.

"You can't hurt it, if that's what you're worried about," she said with confidence.

"How do you know?" He wasn't so sure.

"I've been going to the library and reading everything I can get my hands on about being pregnant, and that topic is more than covered. Didn't think I'd need to know any of it until right now," she said, her tone a low, sexy note. But then, he'd always liked the sound of her voice. His gaze roamed all over her throat, thinking of all the times he'd feathered kisses there. "At least, I hope I need to know that now."

She took another step toward him. Now she was so close that he could reach out and touch her. So he did. He took her by the hand and walked her into the bedroom.

By the time he turned around, her hands were already on the fastener of his jeans. He shrugged out of his shirt and then helped her with his pants. Those landed in a pile on the floor along with his boxers.

And then their mouths fused as hands roamed. He cupped her breast, and he could feel her nipple bead against his palm as she gasped. He rolled her nipple between his thumb and forefinger, and she released a sexy moan against his lips.

Her hands were all over his chest and then his arms, his back.

He followed the curve of her hip until her sweet bottom was in his hand. She ground her sex against his.

He had the fleeting thought that he should pull a condom from his side table. Guess it was a little too late for that. The thought of being inside her without a barrier between them sent a thrill rocketing through his body. He wanted to feel her silky skin.

They stood in the bedroom, moonlight streaming around them. He started with her lips and then roamed down, planting a trail of kisses along her chin. He was prepared to take his time even though his body hummed with an urgent need for release.

"I don't think so," she said, tugging him onto the bed. She had other ideas about the pace.

He supported his weight with his knees and

arms as she wrapped her legs around his midsection. Her fingers curled around his erection, and he had to refocus so this whole thing didn't end before it even got interesting.

She guided his tip inside her, his tongue plunging in her sweet mouth as his erection dipped into her sweet heat. Her body tensed and he immediately pulled out.

"What's wrong?" He searched her face for signs of pain, panic beating his chest.

"Nothing. It feels a little too good. I told you that pregnancy hormones intensify everything, didn't I?"

"Yes." He remembered that she did.

"Well, I've been thinking about doing this with you for months, Ryder." Her hand was already guiding him back inside her...home. "You have no idea how much I need this."

Now it was his turn to tense. She was already wct for him. He eased his length inside with a groan as he teased her heat. He went as slowly as he could manage under the circumstances.

She stretched around him and he nearly exploded.

She matched his stride, stroke for stroke, until they worked into a frenzy of heated breaths.

And then she detonated around him, her

body clenching and releasing, so he rode to the edge. He let himself think about how amazing she felt with that silky skin squeezing him.

With a final thrust, his entire body tensed and he exploded inside her.

She felt so damn good.

He didn't pull out right away as his erection pulsed until every last drop drained.

It might've been a costly mistake to look in her eyes right then, but he did it anyway. And he saw something mirrored in them that looked a lot like love.

Rather than overanalyze the emotion coursing through him, Ryder rolled onto his back and pulled Faith close. She fit perfectly as she turned on her side and threw her leg over his. Her head rested on his chest and his heart clutched.

This was going to hurt later.

For now, he planned to let himself get lost in the moment.

FAITH WOKE TO the smell of breakfast cooking in the kitchen. She stirred, a little sore from last night but the happiest she'd been since walking away from Ryder three and a half months ago.

Hadn't she told her father last night that

there'd be consequences to his actions? She was going to try not to eat those words after spending the night in Ryder's arms. If she was going to go through with her plan, she needed some emotional distance.

There was no way she could let her brain go there…where it was trying to make sex with Ryder a bad thing. It wasn't. Sex with that man was nothing short of amazing. But she could be honest enough to realize that it was also a dangerous thing even if she couldn't allow herself to regret it.

She also knew that it couldn't happen again. Not under any circumstances.

Chapter Nine

"Sit. I'll make something to eat," Ryder said after telling Faith good morning. He handed her a cup of decaf.

"Since when did you start cooking?" Faith asked as she took the offering.

He'd already had the talk with himself this morning that sex was just that, sex. They both needed to blow off steam last night—and they did a damn good job of it—and it was the best way to stem the attraction between them that was driving them both to distraction. There was no way they could have sex again.

"Take a seat." He pointed to the small table and chair.

She did.

"I woke up thinking about what my father said last night," she said. "If he's being blackmailed and he doesn't care about what they're threatening him with, where does that leave Nicholas?"

"Good question. You won't like the first thing that pops into my head if I say it," he said, placing bread in the toaster.

"No. I won't. Because it's the same thing I'm thinking," she replied, and then took a sip of coffee.

"We need to figure out who is behind this," he said.

"Or I could just let them take me. Maybe that's why the guys were trying to kidnap me the other day. Whoever is in charge didn't get the leverage they expected with Nicholas so they decided to up the ante with an actual McCabe. I'm sure they'd take me to wherever Nicholas is being held," she said.

"Absolutely not. No way." He stopped what he was doing long enough to stare at her. "Don't even think about it."

"But he might be in trouble. Maybe I can help," she offered.

"Or maybe you can get all three of you killed."

She drew back with a pained reaction.

"I'm sorry. I'm not trying to be a jerk." Ryder didn't want to be so direct, but he needed her to make herself and the baby top priority.

"I know," she said quietly. "I would never do anything to hurt the little bean."

"If anyone goes in, it's going to be me," he said. "Promise me that you won't do anything without talking it over with me first and giving me a chance to figure out a better move."

She sat there for a long moment thinking. He wasn't sure if she realized that her hand came down over her stomach, but he took it as a good sign.

"You're right, Ryder. I won't be stupid," she said.

"You couldn't be. You're too smart for that. But I could see you running in to save him without taking your own life into consideration," he said. "Your heart is too big and you put yourself last."

"But it's not just my life anymore, is it?" It wasn't really a question, so he didn't answer.

"I keep thinking about my mom. How she's endured so much from my father over the years. It's no wonder she relies on pills. She's been even more anxious lately, and I can understand why. Living with my father has to be getting to her."

Ryder grabbed the pieces of toast as soon as they popped up and then put a dollop of butter on each. "You liked it this way at the restaurant the other morning."

She nodded, smiling.

And that shouldn't make him feel proud of himself for putting a little sunshine on her face.

"I know your mother isn't like him. But you can't give up your life for hers. She made a choice to live with him and you're not responsible for that decision," he said.

Faith took a bite of the toast being offered and chewed on it.

"It's just hard because I've always been her safety net," she said. "Without me, she has nothing. She's the reason I came back from college to live here. I had no plans to stay in Bluff."

"Oh, yeah? Where would you go?" He couldn't imagine not living in Texas.

"There's this place up north that I fell in love with one summer. It's a small town in Michigan on the lake."

"You mean you didn't want to come back here for me?" He pretended that she'd just knifed him in the chest.

And that made her laugh.

That was the second time that morning his chest felt full. As it was, he needed to keep the mood as light as possible, especially since he didn't want her thinking she needed to run off and be valiant. He'd take finding Nicholas seriously but he didn't want her worrying. That wouldn't be good for her or the baby.

"Cut it out. The place actually reminds me of your ranch in a weird way. Everyone's friendly and neighbors know each other. I'm not haunted by my last name there, so no one treats me differently because I'm a McCabe. Not like here in Bluff." She said the last part under her breath.

"People treat you diff—"

She shot him a look before he could finish.

Of course they did. Even he'd had preconceived ideas about her because of her last name. "I never thought about that before. That must've been hard for you growing up in a town so biased against your family. The bias isn't for no reason, though."

"Of course not. I can see my father for the person he is now. All hope he was a better man came crashing down around me last night. Plus, pretty much everyone around here wants to be an O'Brien," she shot back, and he could tell that she was only half joking. "My best friend in high school was Susan Hanover, remember?"

"I never understood the two of you being friends after I got to know you better," he said. "She was always so manipulative, and that made me think you were the same."

"How many friends do you think a McCabe has in Bluff?" she asked, like he should've figured that out already. "It wasn't exactly easy growing up here with my family name. Don't get me wrong. We didn't go hungry and I'm grateful for small miracles. Plus, I had no idea what my father was truly capable of back then so I thought we were being targeted unfairly." She blew out a burst of air. "Little did I know."

She had a point. It must've been hard to grow up the only decent McCabe, and that was probably the reason she felt so close to Nicholas and protective of her mother. Ryder was beginning to have a better understanding of why she was so motivated to help out her little brother. "I'm gathering that you and Nicholas share a special connection."

"He's the most like me. The only brother I have anything in common with," she said. "I now know that there are others out there based on what I saw last night. I have no idea how many or who they are but there are more."

"One step at a time, okay?" he asked, seeing that her stress levels were picking up again. He pulled on all his self-discipline to keep a little distance between them and not repeat last night.

"I heard about what Susan did to Dallas," she said.

"Trying to peg him as the father of her son to keep her boy safe was wrong on every level, but I can understand a mother's desperate need to protect her child," he said.

"The funny thing that she didn't realize was that all she would've had to do was ask any one of you for help and you would've done whatever you could. It's just the way O'Briens are built," she said, and his chest filled with pride at the admiration in her voice.

"Susan doesn't think like a normal person," he said. "And I'm not a knight in shining armor. I've been a jerk plenty of times when I should've been a shoulder to lean on instead."

His cell phone buzzed.

"I have no idea who this is," he said when he checked the screen.

"Do you have any news?" the familiar voice started, and Ryder knew right away who was on the line.

"It's Celeste," Ryder said to Faith, holding his hand over the mouthpiece.

"Why did you take off the other day?" he asked Celeste.

"I was done talking. I reported Nicholas as missing, like you said," she responded. "Have you found out anything on my boy?" Lack of sleep and worry deepened her voice. She had that low smoker's quality and he figured stress had her doubling up on cigarettes.

"We're still digging around, but we know very little," he said. "We believe that a girl by the name of Hannah was recruited to target him at a place called Wired."

When no hint of recognition came, he added, "Here, let me put you on speaker so we can both explain."

"Is *she* there right now?" Celeste said.

"Yes."

"I didn't call to talk to her," she said bitterly.

"Okay. Just me and you, then," he said, not wanting to scare her off. "Wired is a gaming center where the kids go to connect and play popular computer games."

That must've sounded familiar because she grunted an acknowledgment. He nodded toward Faith, who was leaned forward with all her attention on him.

"The sheriff said he'd let me know if they found anything. Nothing so far." She sucked in a burst of air. "Sheriff said he can sometimes find missing kids using something about a satellite and a chip in phones. He didn't have no luck with Nicholas's. Sheriff also said that Nicholas hasn't used his phone since eight o'clock the night he went missing."

Ryder shook his head. Faith nodded that she understood there was no good news.

"Like we said before. Most teenagers wouldn't be caught without their cell phones," he said.

"And especially not Nicholas. I used to tease him all the time that that smartphone thing was going to grow out of his fingers when he slept." She sniffed back a tear.

"Faith discovered someone is blackmailing her father in connection with Nicholas's disappearance," Ryder said.

Faith shot him a look that said she wasn't happy with him for telling Celeste.

He'd deal with that in a minute. Celeste had a right to know.

"Figures that jerk would be tied up with this somehow," she said, the anger in her voice booming through the speaker.

"He's not behind it," he said. "We know that for certain."

"But he don't care about Nicholas. That boy could be dead for all Hollister would care. In fact, I'd go one further and say that it would do him a favor for Nicholas to be out of the picture. Then he wouldn't have to worry about me coming after him for support."

"Have you tried recently?" he asked, just in case.

"Not since Nicholas was a baby. Once I figured out that Hollister was just using me I didn't want anything else to do with him or his money. This may sound stupid but he told me that he was going to leave his wife for me. Made all kinds of promises that he probably made to every woman he wanted." There was a wistful and wise quality to her voice now. And Ryder suspected she was on point with all counts.

"Think we can swing by and check out Nicholas's room later?" he asked, hoping they'd find a clue there.

A long pause came across the line.

"I've been over his room and didn't find nothing," Celeste said on a heavy sigh.

"Fresh eyes might help," he said.

Another few seconds passed without a response.

"I guess letting you look around wouldn't hurt. The sheriff's already checked over it and didn't find anything," she conceded. "He didn't say I couldn't let anyone else have a look at it."

"I'd still like the chance," he countered, thinking that it might be time to bring in extra help in the form of a private investigator. Five days missing with no word wasn't a good sign.

"I go in to work at eight. You can come by before then. Just *you*. There's no room for a McCabe in my house," she said, leaving no room for question. "They've done enough to mess up my life."

"Just me," he repeated so that Faith could hear. If it were up to him, he'd bring her with him. He wasn't calling the shots and might just get lucky and find something that could lead them to Hannah or, better yet, Nicholas. But based on Celeste's tone when she talked about any McCabe, Ryder knew better than to push the issue of asking if Faith could go with him. Besides, he couldn't be sure she wouldn't offend Celeste again. Those two women together were fire and gasoline. Maybe he could help smooth some of that over for Faith and figure out a way for them to forge some kind of bond when Nicholas was home safe.

Celeste didn't say goodbye. She just ended the call. Her defenses were up.

"Of course she'll let you come and not me." Faith blew out a frustrated breath. She stood up and then started pacing. "You know, it might be her blackmailing my father for money since he refused support all those years ago."

"Yeah, I thought about that, which is why I asked. She said no. I believe her. I mean, why now?" he asked. "Plus, that doesn't explain the note."

"I don't know how a crazy person thinks," she shot back. "And she could've sent him off to camp for a week and written that herself. What mother doesn't notify the sheriff when her child goes missing?"

Faith was hitting on territory that Ryder didn't want to go over again. It was a dead end. Celeste wasn't involved.

"It might be best if you stay here and get some rest anyway," he said. "I won't stick around any longer than I have to."

Faith flashed her eyes at him. "I hope not. She's a black widow, that woman."

What was going on there? Was she jealous?

He couldn't afford to let himself feel the burst of pride. His new mantra was *stay objective* when it came to Faith. The baby deserved that much from both of them, and getting too attached would only muddy the waters. *Good one, O'Brien.* Like sleeping with her hadn't already done that. He told himself that it wasn't too late to salvage a friendship between them. Anything else had *disaster* stamped all over it. He had no plans to walk into that trap again no matter how right it had felt at the time. And it had felt damn right.

Of course it had. Faith was gorgeous. She was easy to talk to. He liked joking around with her. Naturally, mind-blowing sex would follow. His groin tightened thinking about it. And since there was no chance of a repeat, he said, "I'm going to take a shower. We can talk more when I get out."

WHEN RYDER STEPPED into the kitchen wearing jeans hung low on his hips and no shirt, Faith was determined not to watch a couple stray rivulets of water rolling down his muscled chest. Her fingers stretched, remembering the feel of his skin from last night. She forced her gaze away. Memories were as close as she planned to get to that toned, athletic, silk-over-steel body of his from here on out. Anything else was tempting kerosene with a lit match.

"Thunderstorm's coming," she warned, having checked her phone while he was in the shower. "They're saying it might be a bad one."

"Truck should be okay," he said, gulping down a glass of water in the kitchenette.

"Hope it doesn't get too bad. Route 453 might wash out." She didn't need to remind him there was only one way to the fishing cabin and one way out.

"I'll check before I head back home," he said, his voice a sea of calm.

Meanwhile, she hoped he couldn't hear her heart thundering. Not knowing if Nicholas was okay had her pulse making double time. And then there was Ryder. He'd always had that effect on her. Even when they were teenagers and he acted like he had no idea who she was. That was the only explanation for him smiling at her in the halls. No one else ever did that.

"Be careful out there just in case," she said.

He checked his phone. "Shouldn't be too bad. Believe me, I've driven through worse."

FAITH LOOKED AROUND for a magazine to read in order to pass the time. There were none. She played around on her phone, checking Nicholas's social media pages for the umpteenth time. Waiting for Ryder to return from Celeste's house was worse than watching paint dry.

She glanced down at her belly. A little boredom was worth it for this little bean growing inside her. Unless stress with no foreseeable outlet could actually kill a person, which felt like a very real consideration at the moment.

Now she was just getting punchy.

The sun was starting to fade. It got dark by seven thirty this time of year. Celeste's place was nearly an hour away, and Ryder had said that she left for work at seven thirty for an eight o'clock shift. He'd said that he would call as soon as he could and that he didn't want to upset Celeste by walking through her house with a cell phone glued to his ear.

She'd known he might be back late when he'd gone out and brought back groceries before he left. He'd offered to pick up takeout but Faith had refused. She'd needed something to do, and cooking dinner was busywork even though she didn't know how to make much more than soup and a sandwich.

Her mind wasn't easy to shut down. If she wasn't wringing her hands, worrying about Nicholas, her mind was going to places that she couldn't afford with Ryder. So far, she'd avoided stepping into the bedroom. They'd spent a wild night in there and she didn't need to be reminded of what she'd be missing out on for the rest of her life. Sex with Ryder had been beyond amazing. Her body had needed the release, she tried to tell herself, and it seemed both had regained their senses after getting caught up in the moment and giving in to the heat between them. She'd chalk her desire up to rogue hormones but she knew in her heart that it was more than that. It was Ryder. Tall. Dark. Sexy. Ryder.

Okay, boredom really was taking a toll. There was no TV at the fishing cabin, so she showered, put on another one of Ryder's old T-shirts, and then wrapped herself in a blanket to sit on one of the rocking chairs out on the porch. There was a chill in the air tonight, and the weather app on her phone had predicted a nasty thunderstorm would be rolling in soon.

As she sat outside and felt the breeze in her hair, she saw the first wave of thick dark clouds forming as the sun dipped into the shadows across the horizon. Flash flooding could be a big problem this time of year, and she prayed that Ryder wouldn't get caught out in one as the first droplets of rain fell. He should be fine in his truck. He'd driven through much worse, she reminded herself.

The thought of being stuck at the cabin, alone, didn't sit well. She wouldn't risk driving if the weather turned out as bad as predicted. Of course, growing up in Texas she'd learned to take weather forecasts with a grain of salt.

Sitting on the porch, she was beginning to give in to her fears that the situation was completely hopeless. Was there any way to get back into the ranch unseen so she could dig around a little more?

No. Her father was smart enough to find a better hiding place for the documents. He wouldn't risk Faith alerting her mother to what was going on. He wouldn't jeopardize what he already had. Thinking about her mother, how lost and alone she'd looked last night, brought fresh guilt washing through her. There was something else about her mother that had changed recently, too. Or maybe it was just stress catching up to her.

Experience had taught her that her mother most likely woke this morning with no recollection of what had happened last night and that was probably for the best. Maybe she could get a message to her mother before she left town. Some note to let her mother know that Faith was going to be okay rather than leave her to worry.

The air pressure changed and a wall of humidity hit as the hairs on the back of Faith's neck pricked. She searched the nearby tree line, trying to stem the creepy-crawly feeling that someone was watching her as large droplets of rain splotched the partially covered porch.

Lightning struck and thunder rocked.

Faith gathered her blanket around her and dashed inside to get out of the downpour. She peeked out the window, looking for any sign of headlights. It was getting late and there was no sign of Ryder. She checked her cell phone. No bars. The storm must be interfering with the signal. She bit back a curse.

Rain started coming down in sheets, reducing visibility to not much more than the end of the porch. She shivered under the wet blanket.

Thunder cracked and the lights blinked. She could start a fire in the fireplace in case she lost power. That would provide warmth and light.

She shrugged off the blanket and loaded a couple pieces of wood. She'd noticed a set of long matches in the kitchen earlier and she needed to find paper for tinder.

As she turned, she heard the wood floor groan behind her. By the time she registered an intruder, some kind of cloth was over her head and something like a rope was being tightened around her neck.

She tried to drop to the floor to break free from the viselike hands on her arms, but she was immediately hoisted back up. The hands were the size of a male's and she heard grunting noises as the men worked. There had to be at least two of them, one holding her upright and the other working the bag over her head.

Panic roared through her, robbing her breath. *Breathe.*

Before she could get her bearings she was being hauled off her feet. She twisted, trying to get them to drop her. These men were far stronger than the ones from the SUV. Bolder, too, she thought, given that they'd come to the O'Brien fishing cabin.

Faith screamed and fought even though there was no one around for miles to hear or help her.

Neither man spoke and all she could hear over the pounding rain was the sound of her own heartbeat. No matter how hard she twisted, there wasn't much give. The men who were taking her were strong. She remembered the threat that had worked so well earlier. But then, if these men were hired to take over for the others, they wouldn't care whose cabin this belonged to. Angering an O'Brien would roll off their backs. And she wondered who'd be crazy enough to do that.

Since her earlier attempts to break free had been fruitless, she needed to calm herself enough to bide her time. If she saw an opportunity, she'd run like hell. In the meantime, she'd conserve her energy. No way would she risk anything happening to little bean.

Fear rocketed through her body as she heard something scraping against the wood floors. And then suddenly she was being forced into a sitting position as her arms were being jacked up behind her body. Some kind of wire or thin rope was being twirled around her wrists, and real fear ripped through her. Terror squeezed her chest, making her lungs hurt.

Her fear of being abducted shrank as her feet were bound together and then tied to the chair. These guys had no intention of leaving with her. She had no idea what would happen next. Would they shoot her? Stab her? She grimaced, tensing her body as she expected the worst to hit at any second. Not knowing what would happen was far worse than any physical torture they could've done.

She strained to hear over the battering the cabin was taking from the rain. Feet shuffled across the wood. And she realized that the sound was…moving away from her?

What on earth?

Every muscle in Faith's body tensed as she waited for the men to return. Or worse yet, were they bringing in someone else to kill her?

Her heart battered her ribs as she tried to breathe slowly. Tremors rocked her body. She needed to get her blood pressure down. It was pitch-black as she felt around, trying to work the bindings on her wrists. It was no use.

She tried not to think about all the ways in which these men could do away with her. Calming her racing thoughts was next to impossible. It was impossible to hear anything over the rain on the tin roof. Impossible not to let fear grip her.

Faith prepared for the worst. Of course, there was the slight possibility that they'd take her to the same place Nicholas was being held. But then, wouldn't they have done that already?

What kind of torture was being planned that would take this long to prepare?

A door closed. Faith stilled, listening for footsteps.

There were none.

This couldn't be it. Could it?

Chapter Ten

Ryder couldn't reach Faith on his way back to the cabin and he could admit that put him on edge. Making the drive out to Celeste's had netted a whopping zero, and now there was a tree trunk blocking the turnoff to the fishing cabin thanks to the storm. Not exactly the makings of a good day.

He jumped out of his truck and shivered in the freezing cold rain. Ryder could do cold or he could do wet. He couldn't do cold *and* wet.

Twenty minutes later, he returned to his seat soaked to the bone but with a clear road ahead. Water poured from his body as he put the gearshift into Drive and pressed the gas, taking it slow. He didn't want to risk getting stuck somewhere along the two-mile drive and have to hike his way to the cabin. It was too cold and he was drenched as it was.

His mood was pretty sour by the time he

parked and cut off his lights. Either Faith was asleep, which he doubted, or the power was out. A common occurrence at the fishing cabin when it rained. And it had come down in sheets earlier. He took the porch steps two at a clip, opened the door and hit the light switch.

"Faith?" He rocketed toward the female figure strapped to a chair in the middle of the room with a cloth sack over her head.

"Ryder, stop!" The words came out desperate, freezing him in his tracks. "They might still be here. Watch out!"

He scanned his surroundings as he backtracked to his truck to retrieve his shotgun. Anyone hanging around the cabin was about to get a big surprise. The fact that no one had jumped him so far made him believe whoever had done this was long gone, but there was no chance in hell he was planning to risk it.

After taking the sack off Faith's head, shotgun resting on his right arm and ready, Ryder pulled a knife from the kitchen. Ever alert, he sliced through the rope binding Faith's arms.

Moving around to face her, he put his index finger to his lips and motioned toward her ankles before placing the knife across her lap so that she could free herself.

There was only a bedroom, bathroom and

closet to search. He checked the closet last, moving around the bed looking for any other spot where someone could hide along the way.

Faith joined him, rubbing her wrists, and he tucked her behind him as he finished with the bathroom.

The place was clear, so he locked the front door. He didn't bother lowering the shotgun and had no plans to until he got her out of there. He turned and hauled her against his chest.

"Are you okay?" he said in almost a whisper. A quick visual scan didn't reveal any signs of injuries. Her wrists were red and he figured her ankles would be, as well. He walked her toward the couch.

Faith sat on the edge, looking too stunned to speak. Ryder brought her a glass of water. There was something on her lap and she was staring at it.

The burlap sack. And words. There were words scribbled on the burlap sack that had been placed over her head.

Leave it alone.

It was a warning delivered by bullies.

He seethed with anger at the thought anything could've happened to her while he was away.

"We can't stay here," Ryder said to Faith.

She nodded blankly.

"I'm taking you where I know I can protect you," he said. His voice was calm but left no room for doubt that there'd be no arguments. And he didn't expect any under the circumstances. As it was, she seemed to be in shock.

She looked up, her eyes wide and fearful. "Get me out of here, Ryder."

He didn't bother gathering up their things. Everything they needed was at the ranch, including better security than at the county lockup. Tommy had advised their parents on all aspects of security given that there were a lot of poachers in the area.

The rain was pounding the roof as Ryder closed and then locked the front door. All he could think of was that this had just become personal. The fight had been brought to his doorstep. And he had no intention of backing down.

"Why would they do that?" she finally asked when he'd secured her inside the truck. "I thought they were going to kill me and then they just left."

"Someone is warning you but they don't want you dead," he said.

"What kind of person does this?"

"They were showing us that they could get to you if they wanted," he finally said after taking his seat and thinking about it. "And that makes me think that whoever took Nicholas is keeping him alive."

"I felt at least two sets of hands on me. I tried to fight but they were too strong," she said, staring out the windshield, unmoved by the wipers' rhythm. "I was too surprised."

"Whoever is behind this might have been watching you for a few days. You said your father had pictures of you and Nicholas. This might be his twisted way of telling you to walk away," Ryder said, navigating onto the farm road.

Faith sucked in a burst of air. "I hadn't thought about the fact that my father might've been behind this attack. The whole time they were there—" she paused "—and it couldn't have been more than fifteen minutes in total, my mind was racing and I kept trying to figure out who would hurt me. Who would want me killed? Not once did I think of my father. And yet it makes perfect sense now that they walked away. I need to get my mother out of there and away from that lunatic."

"One step at a time. Your mother's safe as long as she doesn't stand up to him or get in his business."

Faith didn't think before she answered. "She won't. I can assure you of that. She's never gone up against that man a day in her life. I think she's too afraid of him."

"Then she's okay. Right now my only concern is you." Yes, he cared deeply about what could've happened to the baby but he couldn't think about that right now. Without Faith, there was no child.

No more unnecessary risks. Not on his watch. It was high time he brought in reinforcements.

"No one's truly safe in my family," she said through a low sob.

"Did you get a look at the men who did this to you? Anything at all?" Ryder asked.

"No. I was about to make a fire and then… *boom*. A bag was being shoved over my head and I was being picked up. I tried to fight back but they were strong. It all happened so fast that I didn't see anything and neither of them said a word. All I heard was a little bit of grunting when I tried to twist out of their grip. That's it. I have nothing to go on."

"Once we get to the ranch, I'll call a family meeting and we'll put our heads together," he said, gripping the wheel a little tighter.

"Do you have to bring everyone in?"

"I won't put anyone in my family at risk without their knowledge." He turned the wheel, navigating onto the road, watching to see if anyone followed.

"Is there anywhere else we can go then? There's already enough at stake and I'm pretty much the last person any O'Brien wants to see."

"That's not true. I'm here and I want to see you," he said, and he meant it. He cared about her, and the entire situation she was in with her family struck a bad chord. Even though he'd retreated into himself after his parents' murders he always knew that his family would be there if he needed them. Everyone might've processed the news differently but they were all on the same page when it came to support. "My brothers aren't going to treat you any differently than they would anyone else. If I bring you onto the ranch, they'll accept you being there."

"I can't begin to fathom that kind of loyalty," she said so softly he almost couldn't hear.

Being a McCabe had taken a toll on her. He had a fleeting thought that his child would never know that brand of rejection. Speaking of children, Ryder didn't like the fact that it had been five days since anyone had seen or heard from Faith's brother. "I need to touch base with Nicholas's mother and maybe get her out of town for a few days. I didn't find anything in his room and she's in danger."

"He'll hurt her, won't he?" Faith finally said.

"It's a possibility we can't ignore," Ryder said. The fact that Faith had been strongly warned but not injured pointed toward her father being behind what had happened tonight. As difficult as that was for Ryder to fathom, he figured he'd never understand the actions of Hollister McCabe and it was best not to underestimate the man.

Her hand came up to cover her stomach and he wondered if she even realized she did that every time she worried about the possibility of something happening to the baby. Faith was going to be a good mother.

RYDER HAD BRIEFED Tommy on the situation on the way to the ranch. Dallas and Austin were on their way. Joshua, Ryder's twin, was the first to arrive.

After a bear hug greeting, Ryder motioned toward the kitchen where a fresh pot of coffee had just finished brewing.

"What's going on?" Joshua asked.

"We'll wait for the others to arrive before we talk," Ryder started, "but you should know that this involves Faith McCabe."

Ryder's back was turned while he poured two cups of coffee, so he didn't see his brother's reaction to the news and that was probably for the best. He wasn't lying before when he'd said that his brothers would accept anyone he brought through that door. However, it would take some time for them to warm up to a McCabe.

If Joshua was shocked, he'd recovered by the time Ryder turned around. His brother took the mug he handed to him. "You know me. I'm up for pretty much anything as long as it's legal."

Joshua's grin was wide. Ryder knew his twin well enough to realize that he had questions—questions he was holding back.

"I know I have a lot of explaining to do," he offered.

"Well, this had better make for a good campfire story someday," Joshua quipped.

Ryder couldn't help but chuckle. "Believe me when I say that people around town will be chewing on this one for a long time when word gets out."

"Well, good. Maybe they'll stop talking about me and Tyler," Joshua teased, Tyler was one of their older brothers who'd recently had a scrape with criminals. Joshua was in the process of planning his wedding to Alice, a single mother with young twin boys and a teenage daughter they were planning to adopt.

"We've had more than our fair share of excitement on the ranch," Ryder said.

"That and a baby boom," Joshua retorted.

Ryder let that one go without a reaction.

Dallas and Austin arrived together before Ryder finished his cup of coffee.

"We saw Dr. McConnell's truck parked out front. You all right?" Dallas asked after a bear hug. The doctor was a good friend of the family.

"I'm good. It's not me," Ryder said. He'd convinced Faith to allow their family friend to examine her. Surprisingly, Faith hadn't put up a fight. The doctor had been in the guest room with Faith for longer than Ryder was comfortable.

He motioned for his brothers to follow him into the kitchen area.

"Either of you want a cup of coffee?" he asked as they greeted Joshua.

"I'll get it," Austin said after hugging his brother.

Ryder pulled Dallas to the side. His brother might not be thrilled that Faith McCabe was involved given that her onetime best friend,

Susan, had tried to manipulate him into marriage and then claimed he was the father of her child. All of which turned out to be a ruse because she'd ended up in a relationship with a criminal. And Dallas deserved a chance to back out of this situation gracefully.

"I just want you to know the players involved and if you need to walk on this one, I'll understand," Ryder said to Dallas.

"If it involves you, I'm in. I don't need to know any other names," Dallas said without hesitation.

"Faith McCabe is in my guest room," Ryder said.

"Okay," Dallas said, unmoved. He started to say something else when Dr. McConnell walked into the room.

All four brothers stopped to hear what she had to say.

Dr. McConnell found Ryder. "You want to take this outside?"

"No. I'd been planning to tell my brothers anyway. Now's a good a time as any," he said.

"The baby looks good. Faith is tired, scared. She needs rest and no more stress. But everything should be fine. I still want to see her in my office tomorrow morning," Dr. McConnell said. "But I'm not seeing anything of concern."

Ryder released the breath he'd been holding.

"Thank you," he said to the doctor.

"If she has any more bleeding or cramping, I want to know right away," Dr. McConnell said.

"She's bled before?" Ryder asked.

"It can be perfectly normal. I'm ordering bed rest for the next few days.

"Will do, ma'am," Ryder said, and then showed her out the door after an exchange of hugs.

He returned to a silent room.

"Everyone knows what we've been through in the past year, so there's no need to rehash those tragic events. Faith and I started seeing each other during that time and now we're going to have a baby," he said, looking for a reaction from his brothers.

Calm-faced, they gave away nothing.

"Let me be the first to congratulate you both," Dallas said after a thoughtful pause. "Having Jackson is the best thing that ever happened to me, and I know you'll make a great dad."

The other brothers chimed in with similar sentiments.

"When did you find out?" Joshua asked first.

Ryder glanced at the date on his watch. "Two days ago."

"Is she in trouble with the law?" Dallas asked.

"No." Since Tommy had already been updated on the phone, Ryder figured it was okay to tell his brothers what was going on. "Faith has a fifteen-year-old half brother who disappeared five days ago. His mother works as a cocktail waitress a couple of counties over and she thought teenage hormones had gotten the best of him. According to Faith, he's a good kid. Not like the other McCabe boys. To make a long story short, her father denied paternity after the kid was born and wormed out of child support. His mother has been struggling to make ends meet ever since. Speaking of Nicholas's mother, I need to send someone from security over to pick her up. She could be in danger."

"You got an address?" Joshua asked.

Ryder pulled it up on his phone and handed the device over to his brother.

"I'll send Gideon to pick her up," Joshua said, referring to their head of security.

"Thank you," Ryder said before continuing. He could already see that it was going to make a huge difference to have full O'Brien support moving forward. "Faith confronted her father. He denies being involved but he mentioned being blackmailed."

"That doesn't exactly narrow down the suspect list," Austin stated. His brother was right.

"Exactly," Ryder agreed. "Faith and I have been investigating on our own while staying at the fishing cabin. Earlier, during the storm, someone broke in while I was away and tied her up. Did their level best to scare her away from continuing to poke around."

Dallas's jaw clenched. His brothers had similar reactions. There wasn't an O'Brien who would take something like that lightly.

"Whoever did this wrote a note on the bag they put over her head." Ryder unfolded the small sack that he'd placed on the counter.

"They could've killed her but they didn't," Joshua said, rejoining the conversation after making the call to Gideon Fisher.

"Why warn her to stop?" Dallas said. "They had her right where they wanted her and they could've silenced her permanently."

"Maybe they don't want blood on their hands. They're small-time," Joshua reasoned.

"Which gives me hope that Nicholas, her brother, is still alive," Ryder said.

All the men agreed.

Faith appeared at the entrance to the hallway. She stood there as stiff as if she was in front of a firing squad. It probably didn't help that all eyes flew to her.

Her tense posture eased a bit as Ryder moved beside her.

Dallas spoke first. "On behalf of all the O'Briens, congratulations."

The others chimed in, saying essentially the same thing. She smiled timidly. It was one of the few moments that Ryder felt that her guard was coming down.

"Do you want anything? Water?" he asked quietly.

"No. Thanks. I'm okay. I'm interested in hearing what's going on in here," she said with a small smile.

Joshua spoke first. "Someone is trying to scare you. This is a message telling you to back off."

"Good point." Dallas had started pacing.

"All we know so far is that a female is in charge," she said. "My father hasn't been faithful to my mother over the years and I'm sure he's hurt many women."

Ryder held a hand up. "We were followed after our first visit to Nicholas's mother. Two men abducted Faith at a gas station when I was inside the store. I went after them and as soon as Faith told them an O'Brien was involved they stopped in the middle of the road and let her go. Tommy knows about what happened. In fact, he's on his way over right now. I'm hoping he'll have some kind of information from the Braxton sheriff."

"So, it's someone who has ties to Bluff. Good luck with Sheriff Bastian. He isn't known for sharing," Joshua said. He had been law enforcement in Colorado before returning to Bluff to take his rightful place on the ranch.

Ryder nodded. "Celeste filed a missing persons report and Tommy said that nothing has come across his desk."

"No Amber Alert?" Joshua asked, sounding a little surprised. "Five days is enough time."

"Nothing," Ryder said.

"Which makes me think that the sheriff isn't taking this too seriously," Joshua agreed.

"So, this leaves us where?" Dallas asked. "We have an attempted abduction that gets nixed when they hear an O'Brien is involved."

"Faith had never seen the men before and they obscured their faces with scarves." Ryder said.

"All I remember is seeing dark eyes. The driver was wearing sunglasses so I saw even less of him," Faith supplied.

Ryder's cell phone buzzed. He pulled it out

and checked the screen. "It's a text from security. Tommy's here."

A few minutes later, Tommy was knocking on the door.

"I got this." Joshua answered the door and then ushered him into the kitchen.

"Any news out of Braxton?" Ryder asked.

"I just got off the phone with the sheriff," Tommy started, looking from Faith to Ryder.

Ryder put his arm around her without thinking and pulled her closer to him.

"Three bodies turned up this morning. All I'm being told is that they were found shot to death in a forest green SUV," Tommy said.

Chapter Eleven

Ryder tightened his grip around Faith as he absorbed the news. Even though the men weren't walking on the right side of the law, they'd done the right thing in letting Faith go. They didn't deserve to die. And then there was Nicholas to consider. Up until now, Ryder had counted on the fact that no one had been hurt. Faith had been in harm's way twice and had been released, which had everyone believing this group was into scare tactics.

This news changed everything. The third body could be Nicholas's.

"Did the sheriff in Braxton mention anything about my brother?" Faith asked. Chin up, determination in her eyes.

"An Amber Alert has now been issued and he's stepping up his investigation," Tommy said.

That was the first good sign that the third body wasn't male.

"What can we do to help?" Dallas asked.

"Right now? Something none of you are good at. Hold off and let law enforcement do our jobs," Tommy said.

The comment netted a few grumbles.

"It's my job to advise you of that," he clarified. "As your friend I have to tell you to be careful not to get in the way of the investigation."

"We have an issue that needs to be dealt with," Joshua said. "Faith is pregnant, and if word gets out— and let's face it, it always does—then we're going to have trouble on our hands."

"I'm not planning to tell anyone. We're cooperating fully with the Braxton County Sheriff's office and that means looking at everyone here locally who could be involved," Tommy said. He wouldn't be able to share much more than that.

"Any ideas who the shooter was?" Joshua asked.

"None. They're processing the scene now, hoping for fingerprints, but you of all people know how that goes." Tommy referenced the fact that Ryder's twin was former law enforcement.

Joshua nodded.

"We know as much as you do so far. A

random girl by the name of Hannah shows up to Nicholas Bowden's occasional hangout spot. The two get together and then Nicholas goes missing. Hollister McCabe is then contacted with a demand for money or the relationship will be exposed. The question I can't answer is what does your father have to lose?" Tommy asked. He shot an apologetic look toward Faith. "He already has a bad reputation, so he can't be worried about that. Your mother could leave him."

"I highly doubt that. She hasn't left yet no matter what toll his antics take on her. This person might've made the mistake of thinking that my father cared about Nicholas," Faith said with so much sadness in her voice.

"Taking him might've been a warning," Tommy said. "Given that the description of the vehicle matches the one you gave me for your attempted kidnapping, I'm working off the assumption these are the same guys. Which gives me the feeling this whole situation is escalating."

"And what about the men at the cabin?" she asked. "They were stronger."

"The men from the SUV refused to take you based on an O'Brien being involved. They might've gotten scared and threatened to go to law enforcement," Tommy stated.

"Which could be why they were killed," Joshua added. "Whoever is behind this might be doing cleanup work."

"Could other McCabes be in danger?" Faith asked.

"Seems like the men from the cabin would've taken you," Tommy said.

Dallas, who had been listening patiently, said, "My gut is telling me these kidnappers are right under our noses. This is personal. They know us, or of us."

Tommy agreed.

"Which would also lead me to believe whatever your father did had to be recent," Ryder said. "Can you think of anyone he's had conflict with recently?"

"Like business affairs?" Faith asked.

"Could be. It would have to be fairly significant to net this kind of response," Tommy said. "The person behind this might believe they're owed."

"The largest deal my father was involved in was about two years ago and that was the Hattie ranch," she said. "It was bad. My father forced them off their land and I remember him being a little unsettled after. I knew then that he wasn't struggling with a bout of conscience. I think the sons threatened him."

"Two years would be enough time for people to forget. They might've been biding their time, waiting for an opportunity for revenge," Ryder said.

"They would also be inexperienced at blackmail," Joshua added. "Thus, all the warnings."

"I remember when news of that deal broke. Your father bought out the interests from the bank, and then he foreclosed on them," Dallas said in a neutral tone. "The family left town and disappeared after that. I think Dad even reached out to them to help. Mr. Hattie was proud and said they'd be okay. They'd been through hard times before."

"Weren't there two sons?" Tommy asked.

"I believe so," Dallas stated.

"Anyone have any idea where they went?" Tommy asked.

"I didn't know the family, but then I tend to keep to myself," Faith said. "And it has been a long time. Surely they wouldn't still be carrying a grudge."

"You never know," Dallas said.

"Let's play this scenario out for a minute," Tommy said. "McCabe takes over the Hattie ranch and they disappear. What then? They wait for how long..."

"Almost two years," Faith supplied.

"Two years is a long time to wait for revenge," Tommy said. The small burst of hope they could be onto something fizzled.

"Unless something else happened to trigger a need, right?" Ryder asked. "Or they start working with someone else. A woman who has been scorned by McCabe could've known what happened and recruited them."

"I'll have Deputy Garcia do some digging to find out where they moved and what they've been up to. If there's a catalyst, he might be able to find it," Tommy said. He excused himself and then stepped outside to make the call to his deputy.

He returned a few minutes later. "Garcia is on it, seeing if he can find out anything about the Hatties."

"If the Hattie family is behind this they clearly didn't know my father very well," Faith said. "Or they would've taken one of my brothers. He cares more about those boys than anything else. It's twisted, don't get me wrong. But he'd be heartbroken if anything happened to one of them."

"Whoever did this didn't want to get caught and they might've wanted someone younger, someone who couldn't fight them off as easily," Tommy said after a thoughtful pause. "They tried to make Celeste Bowden believe that her son was disappearing for a few days to punish her. They probably expected to blackmail your father, get whatever they wanted and then return him safely home."

"But my father refused to pay and they started getting desperate," Faith said.

"Then we realized Nicholas was missing and started investigating. They got nervous and tried to snatch you," Ryder added. "But they didn't want to get into too much trouble because as soon as you dropped my name they let you go."

"All signs point to amateurs being involved so far," Tommy said. "And they would fit the bill. We also know there's a woman involved."

"What about the third person who was found in the SUV?" Faith asked, her bottom lip trembling, and Ryder could see how much effort it was taking for her not to cry.

"Let's operate under the assumption that Nicholas is fine until we hear differently," Tommy said. "It's a good sign that the sheriff issued an Amber Alert."

The silence in the room was deafening.

"Okay. So tonight's attack. What does that mean?" Faith asked, rubbing her wrists again.

"You weren't hurt in any way and that's another good sign for Nicholas," Tommy said.

"Except that the people who tried to kidnap me are dead," Faith said.

"Your father refused to pay and plans are falling apart. People are getting desperate," Tommy agreed. "Let's follow the evidence and see where it leads."

"If the kidnappers are starting to panic," Faith said after a thoughtful moment, "that's not good news for my brother."

JANIS BROUGHT FOOD from the main house. There was no way Faith could eat until she knew if her brother was alive. Her nerves were on edge and she jumped every time someone's cell phone buzzed.

Most everyone made small talk while waiting for word from Tommy, who'd been called away for a different investigation. Ryder insisted that Faith stay seated on the couch if she wasn't willing to comply with complete bed rest. Under the circumstances, he seemed to understand why that was currently impossible.

The knock at the door had Faith ready to jump off the sofa. A woman came in with a baby on her arm, and a chocolate Lab followed them both. The mother and child were bundled up like it was Alaska in the dead of winter, and that made Faith smile.

"Who's this guy?" Faith asked Ryder as the hundred-pound Lab came toward her, tail wagging.

"That old boy is Denali," he said, bending down long enough to scratch behind the ears of the big dog who walked straight over to Faith and sat down at her feet.

Ryder was called into the kitchen while Faith took over ear-scratching duty.

After watching the woman peel off layer upon layer of outerwear, Faith recognized her.

"You must be Kate Williams. Congratulations to both you and Dallas. I hear you make a great couple," Faith said, extending a hand as the frazzled mom sat next to her on the couch. Dallas took the active baby from her arms, insisting it was his turn to hold the black-haired boy.

"It's really nice to meet you, Faith," Kate said after shaking hands. The woman wasn't tall but she seemed like the type who could hold her own, and Faith respected that. "I was just thinking how nice it'll be to have another woman on the ranch."

"Oh, we're not…actually…" Faith was pretty sure her cheeks had turned a dozen shades of red.

"I'm sorry," Kate quickly said. "I should know better than to assume. Dallas and I had an unusual courtship to say the least. And it's just that you and Ryder look good together, so I just assumed."

"We're friends," Faith said. "And we're going to have to figure out how to raise a baby together."

Kate looked at her with a slightly raised eyebrow. "That's as good a place to start as any."

Faith smiled, thinking it would be nice to have one genuine female friend. Then again, she didn't plan to stick around once Nicholas turned up, if he turned up. She just prayed that she wasn't about to have to ID a body. She shook off the thought before the walls crumbled around her.

"Your son is adorable," Faith said to Kate, refocusing.

"Thank you. He's nine months old now," Kate said. "I might be able to wrangle him away from Dallas if you'd like to hold him."

"Later?" Faith asked, not sure she was ready for that step. What if she upset him? Or he cried? No matter how much she already felt attached to the little bean growing in her stomach, she wasn't sure she felt prepared to care for a baby. Especially with the parenting examples she'd had.

Kate smiled and gave an understanding

nod. Faith was grateful. She didn't want to turn off a possible new ally.

After the meal was set up buffet-style, Faith was surprised again by the O'Briens when everyone took a seat around the table to eat. It had always been her and her mother at the table. There had been plenty of days when a meal for her mother could be found in a cocktail glass.

She couldn't help but look at Jackson, especially as he was being held by Dallas. The bond between the two of them so evident. Would Ryder seem as natural with their child?

Joshua leaned over to Ryder and Faith could hear the conversation since Ryder kept her by his side.

"Did you hear about Uncle Ezra?" Joshua asked.

"Being brought in for questioning again," Ryder said, nodding. "Has Tommy said anything?"

"Ezra has a solid alibi for the night of our parents' murders," Joshua said.

"He and Aunt Bea were having it out over her chickens again," Ryder added. "I wonder what Tommy thinks he's going to find with Uncle Ezra? Are you questioning whether or not he's a suspect?"

"Tommy can't say one way or another and

I wouldn't expect him to. Gets me wondering what he thinks Uncle Ezra might know," Joshua said.

Ryder's aunt and uncle were notorious for not getting along in a family as tight-knit as the O'Briens. But then, that closeness seemed to have come about because of Ryder's parents, both of whom had reputations for being good, honest people in Bluff. Faith could admit that she held the same high regard for the family. And they'd proved it once again now that everyone they'd broken the news to about the unplanned pregnancy seemed to accept it. The O'Brien brothers may have been shocked at first but they'd adjusted and genuinely seemed concerned about her safety.

The sentiment was almost unrecognizable to Faith. For a split second she wondered if they wanted something from her. It was silly, really, but she'd never seen that kind of acceptance in her own family.

A part of her was relieved that her child would be loved unconditionally by one side of the family. Except that also complicated everything…

No one in her family knew about the baby and she needed to keep it that way. Or be long gone by the time they found out.

Nothing was going according to plan. She'd

been holding back from leaving so that she could spend as much time with Nicholas as possible before she disappeared.

Thinking about family had her wondering about her own mother. Did she wake up wondering where Faith was? What would her father say to her? Anything?

Faith tugged on Ryder's hand and then flashed her eyes at him when he looked at her.

"You're worried about your mother, aren't you?" Ryder asked in a low voice.

"Yes," she admitted, thinking the strong connection she had with Ryder was odd to say the least. He knew her better than her own family even though they'd really only known each other for a short time. *Really* known each other and not just preconceived notions they'd had growing up in the same town because she was a McCabe and he was an O'Brien.

Ryder's cell phone rang. The room went dead quiet.

"It's Tommy," he said and then put the call on speaker after informing the sheriff.

"The Hattie family moved outside of San Antonio after losing their land to the McCabes. Once they left Bluff, the family declined. Their two sons, Douglas and Shaw, have criminal records for petty crimes in the past year. Turns out, they got involved in stealing cars and home invasions," Tommy said. "They're racking up quite a record. Shaw has a girlfriend who fits Hannah's description." There was a pause and voices could be heard in the background. "Hold on," Tommy said. "I have a positive ID on the bodies found in Braxton County this morning."

Faith held her breath, fearing this would be the news that she'd been dreading ever since Nicholas had gone missing. Even Ryder's comforting hand couldn't stop her body from shaking.

"Douglas and Shaw Hattie have been confirmed," Tommy said. "The third victim fits the description of Hannah."

Faith's breath came out in a sharp gasp.

She didn't have a chance to digest the news before Celeste walked through the door with Gideon, the head of O'Brien security. She faintly heard the call with Tommy being ended in the background.

"Why am I here?" Her eyes were wild, and fear was stamped all over the worry lines of her face.

"It's for your safety," Ryder said. "We have reason to believe you might be in danger."

"Oh." She thought about that for a moment. Her gaze intensified. "I'm taking it that you still haven't found my boy."

"No. But the men we believe were involved in his kidnapping have been found dead," Ryder said. "And so has the girl who lured him away."

Celeste gasped and her hand flew to her chest above her heart.

"We're doing everything we can to find your son," Ryder reassured. "So is our sheriff as well as Braxton's."

She gave a nod as she struggled against the tears welling in her eyes. Faith understood the mixed emotions that seemed to be running through Celeste, because she was feeling all of those and more. Relief that Nicholas wasn't dead. Scared that the people who'd abducted him had locked him up somewhere and he'd die of starvation or dehydration now that they were gone. Frightened that whoever killed them now had her brother. Faith absolutely knew that he would make contact with her if he was able.

"Can we talk outside?" Faith asked Celeste, knowing that walking into a room full of O'Briens was most likely overwhelming enough for her even before she heard the news.

Celeste didn't immediately respond. Her gaze bounced from Ryder to Faith before she nodded.

Faith ignored the look from Ryder, the one

that worried she wouldn't be delicate with Celeste. After seeing the panic in the woman's eyes, Faith was starting to accept how much Celeste loved Nicholas. She could work with that and try to put the past behind them, if Celeste could. Besides, seeing Jackson had brought up all of Faith's fears that she wouldn't know what to do with a child, and for the first time, she could sympathize with a woman who had no financial backing and no emotional support. Nicholas could've done a lot worse.

The chilly air goose-bumped her arms as Faith led Nicholas's mother onto the back patio. She welcomed the cold but picked up a quilt for Celeste on the way out. The sky was cloudless and stars shone bright against the canopy of cobalt blue.

"You want to sit?" Faith motioned toward the rocking chair. A matching chair nestled on the other side of a small table. As crazy as the evening had been, Ryder's place felt like home, and she figured it was the small touches like the quilt that made it feel like she belonged there.

Celeste nodded and shivered.

Faith placed the quilt around Nicholas's mother's shoulders. "I'm worried about him, too."

"I didn't want to admit it at first but I can

tell that you care for Nicholas," Celeste said after a thoughtful pause.

"He's the only good thing that ever came from McCabe blood," Faith said, and then added. "And I think that's because he has you."

Celeste's smile didn't reach her eyes and Faith knew why. The woman was worried about her son. Even so, the acknowledgment meant a lot to her.

"It's not a good sign that his kidnappers are dead and they haven't found him yet, is it?" Celeste asked, looking out at the vast sky.

"I'm keeping my hopes up, thinking positive," Faith admitted.

"I've never been so scared before," Celeste said.

"Me, either." There was no reason to hold back. Maybe if Celeste knew how much Faith loved Nicholas she'd agree to let him move to Michigan with her.

"You think something's happened to him?" Celeste asked.

Faith shrugged. "I don't want to allow myself to think like that."

"You got a good man in there," Celeste said, thoughtfully.

"I'm pregnant," Faith admitted, and it felt good to be able to tell someone else. "It's the only reason he agreed to help in the first place. And I blackmailed him into doing it. He didn't know he was a father before I dropped that bomb on him."

Faith was a little baffled as to why she felt the need to confide in Celeste. She'd say that it felt good to talk to someone, anyone, but the truth was that she was beginning to actually like and respect Nicholas's mother—a woman who was bringing up a good young man on a shoestring budget with no support.

Celeste reached out and took Faith's hand in hers and the two sat quietly for a long time. It was a peaceful silence, a camaraderie that Faith had never felt before with another woman. A few moments ago with Kate on the couch was the closest she'd ever come.

"I've been in that situation before. With my Nicholas. A good man won't walk away," Celeste said.

"Ryder would do the right thing if I let him," she said. "Trapping him is unfair to everyone."

"Then you don't see what I do," Celeste said after another thoughtful pause.

"Yeah? What's that?" Faith asked.

"That man has real feelings for you. If he didn't, he wouldn't be here. He might do the right thing by his own child but he wouldn't be looking for Nicholas, pregnant or not."

"He's a good man. I basically blackmailed him into helping me find Nicholas. What kind of trust is that to build on?" Faith asked, listening for any trace of judgment in the woman's voice. She couldn't find any. There was sympathy and kindness. No judgment. And she felt like a jerk for being so hard on Celeste's parenting. Faith's child hadn't even been born yet and she could already see that none of this was going to be easy. And trying to make ends meet as a single mother who'd had no opportunity had to have been the worst feeling. Was Celeste perfect? No. Neither was Faith. It was time to jump off her high horse and keep her feet on the ground. See the truth.

"I can see why you'd think that," Celeste said. "And no one wants to feel like a man married them because he was forced to. There's nothing in that man's eyes that makes me think he wouldn't have helped you if you'd asked, baby or not."

Faith let that thought simmer. Could it be true? Or was she tempted to believe what she heard because she was pregnant and wanted to give her baby a family? Her hormones were so far out of whack she couldn't decide one way or the other.

"You've been a good mom to him," Faith said after a few minutes.

"I have not been anything of the sort," Celeste snorted. "I've done my best, don't get me wrong, but—"

"Nicholas is a great kid," Faith countered. "That didn't come from my side of the family."

Celeste looked up at the stars, seeming to contemplate what Faith had said. "You turned out all right."

Faith's cell phone buzzed before she could thank Celeste. She squeezed her hand and Celeste seemed to understand what that meant before Faith let go and fished her cell phone out of her pocket.

There was a text from her mother. Faith's heart skidded as she read:

I know what's going on with your father. I can help.
Meet me at Farmer's Mill Road. You know where.

At the end of Farmer's Mill Road was a cornfield where her mother had taken Faith and her brothers the first of every October to kick off the Halloween season when she was a kid. There were hayrides and a pumpkin patch at the mouth of the corn maze. Her brothers had always immediately broken off, running into the maze and jumping out to scare her, except for Jesse. He was the closest thing to a decent McCabe boy, and he seemed the most sympathetic to their mother. She hoped that he would take care of their mother once Faith disappeared.

"I need to show this to Ryder," Faith said. "You coming inside?"

"In a minute," Celeste said. "I like it out here."

Faith put her hand on Celeste's. "Thank you for what you said before."

"It's true. I meant every word."

"That means a lot to me," Faith said, wiping away a stray tear. "When we get Nicholas back, I'd like to be there for both of you." Faith's hand went to her belly. "I have a feeling that we're going to need all the family around we can get."

Celeste practically beamed. It was her first real smile since this whole ordeal had begun.

"We're going to find him and bring him home. I promise," Faith said.

"I hope so. He's my world."

"I know that, too." Faith made a beeline for Ryder the second she spotted him in the kitchen. He was holding baby Jackson, and her heart galloped at the sight.

He looked up and his face morphed as soon as he picked up on Faith's heightened emotions. He handed the boy over to one of his brothers and met her halfway across the room.

"What is it?" he asked.

She showed him her cell phone. "I have to go."

"We'll see what she knows," he said after reading the text. Ryder let everyone know what was happening before he and Faith left in his truck.

"Where on Farmer's Mill Road?" Ryder asked twenty minutes into the drive.

"Remember the corn maze entrance?" she asked.

Ryder nodded.

"We used to go there when I was little," she said. A spark of hope lit that her mother wasn't completely gone. Not if she'd mentioned the mill. The last night with her mother had Faith concerned.

There was a small gravel parking lot at the mill and no other cars.

"We must've beaten her here," Faith said, shivering against the cold as she stepped down from the cab.

"She wouldn't necessarily recognize my

truck. If she knows something, she'll want to be cautious," Ryder said, catching up to her.

"Good point." Faith walked toward the entrance to the maze. It was too cold for corn stalks but the wooden entrance was clearly marked.

"Faith." Her mother stepped from the shadows. "Is that you?"

"I brought Ryder O'Brien with me," Faith said as her mother moved toward her. When she came into the light, Faith could see the bags under her mother's eyes. "I'm so glad you're okay."

They embraced. Her mother felt cold and bony. She was like hugging a skeleton, Faith thought, and there was an emotion present in her eyes that made Faith shiver.

"What's he doing here?" her mother asked. Was that disapproval or disdain in her voice?

Faith started to explain when she felt something hard, something metal press against her ribs.

"No one is going to mess this up for me, you hear?" Mother said and her eyes were wild. "I've lived with that man for thirty-seven years and I've had to endure humiliation after humiliation. Why couldn't you just leave this alone, Faith? It didn't have to be this way. Your father has to pay for what he's done to me. To us."

"You don't want to hurt me, Mother." Faith didn't hide her panic as the pieces clicked together in her mind. Had her mother used and then set up the Hattie boys? Had them shot? She wished there was a way to signal Ryder, who was standing by his truck, giving them privacy. "What have you done, Mother?"

"Everything's spinning out of control and you need to stop digging around." There was a desperate quality to her mother's voice.

"Put the gun down, Mother."

The snick of the bullet being engaged in the chamber dropped Faith's heart. Her mother was serious?

Ryder must've heard because he put his hands in the air as he leaned against his truck. "No one has to get hurt."

"Except maybe they do now because you two wouldn't leave things alone," Jesse said from the opposite direction.

Faith followed the sound of her brother's voice until she saw him. The barrel of her father's favorite Smith & Wesson was trained on Ryder's chest. Reality struck. Was he planning to set up their father for Ryder's murder? For hers?

"You?" Shock didn't begin to cover Faith's

emotions at that moment. Her brother and her mother working together against her father? "What are you doing with Dad's gun?"

"That's right," Jesse said. "You should've listened to our warning instead of dragging the sheriff into it."

Chapter Twelve

"Where's Nicholas?" Faith managed to grind out through the whirlwind of emotions that had to be rushing through her. Ryder could almost see all the neurons that had to be firing in Faith's head with the news.

The Hattie brothers had been worried about a *she*. Karen McCabe.

All Ryder could focus on was the gun pressed against Faith's ribs. His heart stuttered at the thought of it going off. At point-blank range, Faith didn't stand a chance. He had to figure out a way to direct Karen McCabe's gun toward himself instead. He'd take a bullet before he allowed anything to happen to Faith.

"Move over there against the truck," Karen McCabe said to Faith. She took a few bewildered steps toward him before he could reach out to her. He tucked her behind him as best he could, shielding her with his six-foot-three-inch frame.

"Be careful," Ryder warned. "That thing might accidentally go off. You don't want that. You don't want to hurt your daughter."

"I might," Mrs. McCabe said, and her voice had a vacant quality to it.

"It was you all along, wasn't it? You sent those men to the fishing cabin to scare me," Faith said.

Her mother cackled.

"You didn't answer my question. Where is he?" Faith asked with a mix of sadness, anger and hysterics in her voice. She'd underestimated her father, and Ryder prayed she wouldn't make the same mistake with her mother or brother.

"I don't know. Shaw was in charge of that part," Mrs. McCabe said. Her voice was unsteady. She could be on heavy medication. A combination of alcohol and prescription drugs would dim her judgment. Was there anything Ryder could do while Faith was talking, distracting them? He'd had no idea the depth to which the McCabe family would go until that moment—the one where a gun was pointed at one of their own and neither was trying to talk the other one down.

She continued, "Nicholas was only supposed to disappear for a couple of days. Your father was supposed to pay or risk his bastard son being exposed. I thought he'd pay for a son."

"How could you do this to him? He's just a boy and he's good," Faith said.

"He was supposed to be my salvation." Mrs. McCabe was stone-faced. She was too far away for Ryder to make a move for the gun. With Jesse twenty feet to the other side, he'd get off a shot before Ryder could reach her.

Damn.

His shotgun was inside his truck. He couldn't get to it even if there was enough distance.

"I never thought I'd see you with an O'Brien," her mother sneered. "We're not so different, Faith. You'll do anything you have to in order to get out of the family, too."

"Ryder's better than any one of the men in our family," Faith retorted. "Except for Nicholas. He's good. And you've ruined that, too."

This wasn't a good time for her to defend the O'Briens. He shifted position, effectively blocking her line of sight with her mother. He knew full well just how high her emotions would be riding, had to be riding the minute she realized how quickly her mother would likely pull the trigger.

"It's not too late," Ryder hedged. He needed to dig around a little bit and figure out what was going on inside the woman's head if they were going to have a chance of getting out of there alive. "If you let us go and tell us where Nicholas is, you'll never have to see your daughter again. No harm. No foul."

An insidious laugh tore from Mrs. McCabe's throat. "I already said that was Shaw's part, and he couldn't do that right. I should've known better than to involve those idiots. They messed everything up. I can't go back now."

"I'm pregnant," Faith said, and Ryder didn't like the fact that she was playing that card. Based on her mother's reactions so far, she didn't care.

"I know," she said, and it was the first time her voice faltered.

Faith was left speechless, but recovered quickly. "How?"

"I heard you throwing up in your bathroom countless times, Faith. I had four kids, remember? I know the signs of pregnancy when I see them. But I didn't know who the father was until I had you followed," her mother said, and her tone was shaking. Maybe Faith's gamble to mention the baby was paying off.

"Mom, don't do it," Faith pleaded. "Don't hurt us. I'm carrying your grandchild. It doesn't have to be like this. If you're doing all this to hurt Dad, I'm fine with it. He doesn't care about any of us. I'm not the enemy. He is. I'm on your side. I've always been on your side."

A moment of hesitation crossed Mrs. McCabe's features. She looked to Jesse, who shot her an unsympathetic look as he stepped toward them.

"It doesn't matter. We threatened to kill her if he didn't pay and we can't let her walk out of here. He can't think she's alive or we'll get nothing," her brother said.

"Now you're using me as a pawn?" Shock reverberated through her.

"We'll disappear. You can tell him whatever you want about what happened to us." Ryder positioned Faith farther on his right; Jesse was to his left. Mrs. McCabe was dead center in front of them, still too far away to make a move. Maybe if Ryder could get around the right side of the truck with Faith…no, it was too risky. They had two shooters, and he and Faith were unarmed. One of them was likely to get off a decent shot at this range. His money was on Jesse.

"I can't. I have to find my brother," Faith said.

"He's not your family," Mrs. McCabe said.

"Yes. He is. How could you do this to us?" Faith said, and there was so much torment in her voice. "How could you use me? And I can't believe what you've done to the Hattie brothers and that girl. Are you planning to kill me, too?"

"What?" Mrs. McCabe seemed confused.

"The Hattie brothers and that girl," Faith said. Ryder squeezed her hand, warning her not to continue. "They're dead. They were shot."

Her mother's gaze intensified on Jesse as she let out a sob. "We should've just taken you when we had the chance. I thought we could warn you but your brother was right. You just won't let up. Let me tell you something. I won't end up with nothing from that man. I can't. I deserve so much more, and he won't give me a thing if I leave him. I tried all those years ago when you left for college and he tracked me down like I was some kind of animal and he was a hunter. He threatened to destroy me. And I've been waiting so long to have the last say. But you couldn't leave it alone, could you?" Her gaze locked onto Faith. "I didn't want it to turn out like this, Faith. I'm sorry."

"You have options, Mom. It doesn't have to be this way. I have a place where you can hide. I've been putting money aside in an offshore account. Dad doesn't know. You can have it. You can have everything. I set up a new identity and bought a house. If this is about money, you don't have to do this. I'll take care of you. It's perfect. You can have everything, all of it. I won't tell a soul." Faith sounded desperate, like she was pleading not just for her life but the life of her unborn child.

Mrs. McCabe looked tentatively to Jesse again. Faith was making ground. And yet her words were a punch to Ryder's solar plexus. In all the time they'd been together over the past couple of days she hadn't mentioned anything about a fake identity or a new life. And now it made perfect sense as to why she'd been holding back with him. She'd planned to walk away from the start. She wouldn't have even told him about the baby had she not needed his help. She'd been honest enough about that. But he'd believed that they'd made progress toward some kind of future involving a relationship. Just what that relationship would've been, he had no idea. So, she'd been using him the whole time to find Nicholas. And then she'd planned all along to disappear?

No need to jump to conclusions. One conversation could clear all this up.

"We can't risk it. He's a liability," Jesse said, glancing at Ryder. Then he fired his weapon.

Ryder didn't feel the bullet hit his arm as he pushed Faith back a step and toward the side of the truck. His knee buckled and he landed hard on the gravel.

Faith burst out from behind him and made a beeline toward her mother, who had raised her pistol.

From this position, there was nothing Ryder could do to stop Mrs. McCabe, but her shaky hands would help ensure an inaccurate shot. It was Jesse that Ryder had to focus on. Another step toward him and Jesse was close enough to grab. Ryder scrambled onto his knees and then flew toward Jesse, tackling him at the ankles. Jesse came down hard, his shoulder slamming into the gravel, his hand opening. The gun skidded across the gravel drive.

Blood was everywhere. Ryder needed to move fast before he lost too much, and, even worse, consciousness.

At least the gun was too far away for Jesse to grab it. He was clawing his way toward it when Ryder threw himself on top of Jesse. His six-foot-three-inch frame gave him an advantage over the smaller McCabe. However, all McCabe boys knew how to fight.

Jesse whirled around, knocking Ryder off him and onto the gravel. He sucker punched Ryder's bad arm, causing pain to shoot up his arm. Ryder sucked in a burst of air, dug deep and landed a hard fist to Jesse's chin. His head snapped back. Ryder grabbed his throat using his one good hand.

Jesse wriggled out of Ryder's grasp with the aid of a knee to Ryder's groin.

Coughing, wincing in pain, Ryder managed to grab Jesse's thigh. He battled fatigue, fighting to stay alert.

Jesse fired off a punch, landing it in the middle of Ryder's chest. Didn't help the breathing situation, and blood loss was beginning to be an issue. Ryder blinked blurry eyes as Jesse scored a fist to his face.

"I'M SORRY, BABY, but I can't go back."

"He doesn't know it's you. He'll never tie this back to you and Jesse," Faith offered.

"Faith will tell him or the sheriff." Jesse grunted. "If she leaves here, it's over for us."

"Oh, baby. It wasn't supposed to be like this." Her mother hesitated for a split second and then fired a shot.

Faith was close enough to capitalize on her mother's moment of hesitation. She managed to knock her mother's arm, causing the shot to go wide. Faith pushed her mother and the gun tumbled toward the ground.

A sweep of her mother's ankles had the woman on the ground, facedown. Her mother was still frail and Faith had always been the opposite, strong and capable. She'd do anything to save her child.

"Where's my brother?" Faith asked, using her knee to force her mother to stay on the ground, praying that Ryder was holding his own. She didn't dare risk turning away from her mother, even for a second. "You have to have some idea. Where would they have taken him?"

Her mother reached around for the gun.

"I'm sorry, Faith. I never intended for anything to happen to you. Neither did your brother," her mother said, trying to squirm out of Faith's grip.

It didn't matter how sorry her mother was, or her brother. Either one of them would kill Faith in a heartbeat if she gave them the upper hand. They'd already proved that. Her mother was so lost.

No way would Faith allow her mother to hurt her child.

And Ryder? She could only hope that he was okay. She'd heard the gunshot and half expected to see blood running down her shirt, surprised when it didn't. She prayed that bullet had missed Ryder—the man she loved.

"Ryder," she shouted without taking her eyes off her mother.

By now, Faith was straddling her mother and holding her hands down. She couldn't check to see if Ryder was okay, and her heart pounded against her chest so hard she thought it might explode. Nothing could happen to him.

"Tommy's on his way." Ryder's voice sent a wave a comfort through Faith as he dropped to her side and secured her mother with flex-cuffs. "Joshua left a couple of these in my truck the last time he borrowed it."

Faith glanced around to see her brother on his side, his hands flex-cuffed behind his back.

Ryder was breathing heavy, and when she looked at him she saw blood everywhere.

He was sitting on his heels, over her mother, and she panicked when she couldn't see the source of his blood.

"You're shot," Faith said.

"Yep."

She made a move toward him but he pulled

back. Fear assaulted her that he was protecting her from seeing how bad his injuries were.

"Are you hurt?" he asked.

"No. I think I'm fine, actually. Just shaken up," Faith said. He didn't make eye contact.

It didn't take long for a deputy to arrive.

"I'm so sorry, Faith," her mother said, looking just as lost and alone as she had the other night. Tears streaked her cheeks. "I never intended for any of this to happen. For any of this to go so far."

Ryder was leaning against the back of a cruiser, an EMT at work on his arm. Faith waited until he was done.

"I'd still advise you to go to the hospital," the EMT said to Ryder as she approached.

"I'll swing over when I get a chance," Ryder said before offering a handshake. "Still got work to do."

Tommy had arrived and he was standing next to Ryder.

"Nicholas could be anywhere," she said once the EMT walked away. "He might die from dehydration."

"Braxton County Sheriff's office is working on it," Tommy said. "You can ride with me. I'll wait for you in my vehicle."

He nodded toward Ryder as he walked away and Faith wondered what that was all about.

The two had been talking and she figured she was about to find out. Based on Ryder's stony expression, it wasn't going to be good for her. Faith only cared about a few people: Ryder, Nicholas and her baby. And now, Celeste. Two of those could be gone forever.

Ryder leaned against the bumper of his truck, fixed his gaze on a point in the barren cornfield.

"How's your arm?" she asked for lack of anything better to say.

He didn't answer, didn't budge.

"You were planning to leave when we found him, weren't you?" he asked.

"Yes," she said honestly, "but—"

"I can't." He pushed off the bumper and walked away. There was no doubt in her mind that he meant those two words.

Faith had lost Ryder. Nicholas was out there—somewhere—going to die if they didn't find him. Her family was a mess. Her mom and brother were going to jail or a psych ward. And her father, the real criminal in all this, was a free man. There was no one left in the world that Faith trusted. Well, except for Ryder, and she'd messed that up royally. She couldn't blame him. McCabes were toxic and he was right to walk away.

Faith hated deception and lies. She knew

without a doubt that Ryder did, too. She would come clean with him, with herself, with everyone. Living a lie, like her mother had, would only destroy her and everyone she'd ever loved. She had every plan to move away, but not before she found Nicholas and then confronted her father.

With his life hanging in the balance, her brother had to come before everything else. Now that she'd lost Ryder, nothing else mattered more than Nicholas and the safety of her child.

Where could Nicholas be? Without access to water, he wouldn't live three days. The Hattie brothers had been found this morning. Time was a ticking bomb, the enemy, and Faith struggled to conceal the tears streaming down her face.

She stared out the window of the cruiser as Tommy drove.

"Where are we going?" she finally asked.

"Ryder has asked me to take you back to the ranch. He'll stay in the main house," Tommy said quietly.

She expected his family friend to come off as judgmental but he only sounded sympathetic.

"I have all my available resources looking for Nicholas. They won't stop until every stone has been overturned," Tommy offered.

"Thank you," she said, sniffing back tears. She'd blame it on hormones, and that might be partially true, but the thought of losing Ryder forever hit so hard she could barely breathe. If it weren't for the need to find Nicholas, she'd curl up in a ball and cry. "I know my family hasn't been… They're messed up beyond belief. I just want you to know how much I appreciate you for helping me in spite of everything they've put you through over the years."

"Family is as much about who you chose to be with as it is about the blood running in your veins," Tommy said, thoughtfully.

She thought about the fact that he'd grown up practically an O'Brien and she couldn't help but wonder what had happened to his family. He'd moved in with his uncle, a ranch hand on the O'Brien property, when he was a little boy. Faith never knew what had happened to Tommy's family or why it had broken up. All she knew was that he was lucky to have had other people who cared about him as one of their own.

"I sent a deputy to get a warrant to search your parents' place," Tommy said. "We might find something there to reveal Nicholas's whereabouts. I'll keep you posted every step of the way."

"Can't say that I deserve your kindness," Faith said, unsure how she would cope until he was found.

"You didn't do anything wrong. I remember that you were the nicest one in your family," Tommy said. "Like I said, we can't decide who links us genetically. But we can determine who our real family is."

They pulled into the ranch and drove to Ryder's house. Tommy didn't make a move to get out.

"Are you coming inside?" Faith asked.

"Nah. I'm going back to my office so I can dig through the files that come in. See about finding your brother," he said.

"I can't thank you enough for everything you've done already."

Tommy nodded, half smiling. "The door's unlocked and Janis made the place up for you."

Tears streamed down Faith's cheeks at the thought of being inside Ryder's house without him.

"Give him time. He'll come around," Tommy said, sounding hopeful. There was no real conviction in his voice.

"No. He won't. But thank you for saying

that." She closed the door to the cruiser and figured she needed to figure out her next step.

Inside Ryder's place, there was a note signed from Janis. She'd put fresh-baked cookies on the counter and wanted Faith to help herself. There was a meal in the fridge that just needed to be microwaved. All the instructions were there. Faith doubted she could eat anything, but she recognized that starving herself wouldn't be healthy for the baby, either. Maybe she could find a way to get down a few bites if she kept that thought close to her heart.

The feeling of hopelessness was an oppressive weight on her chest. After everything she'd been through to find her brother, he was still missing. Her mother and brother had no idea where the Hatties had taken Nicholas. With the remorse in her mother's voice, Faith knew she would've told her if she'd known his location. Faith had acted quickly before, but her mother could've shot her a dozen times in that parking lot and didn't. And when she finally managed to pull the trigger, she'd missed.

"Everything okay?" Celeste's voice came from the hallway.

"No," Faith said. "It's not."

With those words, the dam broke and a flood of tears rocked her body.

Comforting arms embraced her as she put her head on Celeste's shoulder and gave in to the emotions overwhelming her.

Chapter Thirteen

"My father took everything from them, their land. He took everything that was good about my mother and shattered it," Faith said to Celeste. "That's what started all of this."

Celeste took Faith's hand.

"The Hatties wrote the note and then took Nicholas, thinking you'd be none the wiser. My mother was behind it all," Faith said. "They all figured he'd be home before you even noticed him missing. They thought my father would care. I have to believe that no one wanted Nicholas hurt. But the men who took him are dead along with the girl."

"If that's true and they had no intention of harming my boy, then he's somewhere tucked away safe," Celeste said. "And that means the sheriff or one of his men will find him."

"Everything's a mess because of my family," Faith said on a sob. "They ruin everything they touch."

"I can only imagine what your mother's been through," Celeste said, thoughtfully.

"She believed she could extort money from my father and get away from him. I'm not making excuses for him, for either one of them, but Jesse probably endured the most emotional abuse from my father because he was the oldest. And I think it warped him."

"Sounds like a hard situation to grow up in and one my boy escaped," Celeste said. "I believe Hollister did me and Nicholas a favor by turning his back on us."

"My mom has been fading away all these years. I saw it happening but couldn't do anything to stop it and yet I never imagined it would come to this. She'd take more medication and my brother started drinking heavily. I always wondered why she wouldn't just leave. I guess my father had a hold over her," Faith said. Now that the dam had broken, she couldn't stop unloading.

"He manipulates people and gets what he wants from them. Sounds like your mother finally cracked. Your brother, too," Celeste said. "People can only take so much."

"It's sad what my father's done to our family—" she glanced up at Celeste "—and to others. He destroys everything he touches."

Tears free-fell and Faith didn't have the strength to hold them in any longer.

"He didn't break us," Celeste said. "You and me are too strong. And he didn't break Nicholas. Hollister McCabe might take down weaker people, but he can't touch the three of us. Four counting the little one who's on the way."

"No, he can't."

"Come on. I want to get you into a warm tub," Celeste said.

"I can't—"

"You have to. All this stress isn't good for that little one." Celeste pointed to Faith's belly.

She was right and Faith shouldn't want to argue. Under the circumstances, it was difficult to worry about herself when her brother might be in danger. She needed to think of the little bean growing in her stomach and dig deep enough to find the strength to take care of herself.

"Besides, you'll think better once you wash off all that dirt."

Celeste made a move toward the master bathroom.

"I'm sleeping in the guest room," Faith said.

"That may very well be, but you're soaking in the big tub," Celeste said. "There was a woman here earlier, Janis, and I already asked. She said it'd be fine and put out some of those good-smelling candles for you."

Faith didn't argue. A warm bath sounded good and she figured that she could go over everything that had happened in her mind while she soaked. Maybe figure out a connection or something that might help find her brother. As it was, she was drawing a blank on what to do next. The sheriff had an address for the Hattie brothers and was checking there. And then there were the parents. Another deputy was being sent to speak to them. An Amber Alert had been issued.

Celeste stayed with Faith long enough to fill the tub with water. "I'll be in the next room if you need anything. Don't hesitate to shout."

"I will."

"Okay then." Celeste turned to leave.

"Celeste..."

She turned.

Faith wrapped her in a hug. "Thank you. I don't know how you've managed to comfort me with everything you're going through, too, but I don't know what I would do without you tonight."

"You're welcome, hon. Us tough girls have to stick together, right." She winked.

"Right." Faith could see where Nicholas got his quiet strength from now.

Celeste patted Faith on the back before reminding her that she'd be in the next room if she needed anything. Having an ally was the only comfort Faith had to hold on to. She'd messed everything up between her and Ryder. If she closed her eyes, she could see the look of hurt in his eyes and she understood why he'd feel that way. She'd cut him out of her plans again. Between the two of them, he was going to be far better at communication than her. If they were going to get along for the sake of their child—and really that was the best scenario she could hope for at the moment—then she needed to get better at talking to him about her plans.

She wished he would walk through the door so she could apologize. Okay, not walk through the door right then while she was stark naked in his bathroom, but after she was out and dressed.

Faith slipped into the warm water and put her head on the rolled-up hand towel/makeshift pillow on the side of the oversize tub. There was enough room in here for her and Ryder, but she highly doubted that he'd want to be anywhere near her now or in the future. And that was probably just as well because she'd only been around him for a couple of days—a couple of extreme, intense days—and she could already see how easy it would be to lose her heart to him again. The pain that had followed walking away from Ryder had been the most intense she'd ever experienced. There was no physical ache that compared.

Now he would most likely never want to see her again. They could arrange visitation without ever having to speak. They could communicate through emails or lawyers.

Michigan had never sounded better. Or did it? What had changed in the past forty-eight hours that made it feel more like running away, hiding?

The small bungalow on the lake suddenly felt less like an escape and more like being banished. And that was silly, really. Or was it? Because she figured it had a lot to do with the fact that she might never see Ryder again.

THE CLOCK READ one twenty in the morning and Faith couldn't sleep. Not even a warm bath followed by a glass of warm milk had done the trick.

No Nicholas.

No Ryder.

But there was plenty of stress. She pushed off the covers and stepped into the robe Janis had brought for her. The cotton nightgown had fit perfectly, but it was too cold to walk around in only that.

She wandered into the living room and stopped. Celeste was curled up on the couch, flipping through a horse magazine.

"How are you doing it?" Faith asked. "How are you so calm?"

"Looking after you is keeping my mind busy. I learned a long time ago that it's no good to make yourself sick with worry over things you can't control," Celeste said, sitting up.

Faith took a seat across from her. "Can't sleep."

Celeste smiled and nodded.

"I didn't know he was married at first," she said after a pause. "Looking back, I should've. I was barely twenty at the time. When I found out, he said they had a bad marriage and he was leaving her. I believed every word. What did I know?"

Faith's father needed to pay for all the hurt he'd caused. "I'm sorry for the way he treated you."

"Thank you. I mean it. For everything

you've done for Nicholas." Celeste closed the magazine and set it on the couch beside her. "I hope you don't mind my saying but you're nothing like your father."

"That's the best compliment anyone could pay me," Faith said with a melancholy smile.

The door opened and Ryder walked through. He made a straight line to the kitchen without acknowledging Faith. He gave a nod toward Celeste.

"I put on a fresh pot of coffee a little while ago," Celeste said. "Hope you don't mind."

"Help yourself as long as you're here," Ryder said, pulling a mug from the cabinet and filling it with the brew.

He stopped at the threshold of the living room and looked straight at Faith. "Can I talk to you?"

Celeste got up and stretched. "I'm tired. I'll just go to bed."

There was so much tension radiating off Ryder. He'd showered and washed the blood off him. He was wearing a clean pair of jeans and a flannel shirt rolled up on the left side. There was white gauze covering his left arm and she was grateful that the bleeding had stopped.

Celeste stopped in front of Faith.

"You okay?" she asked.

"Yeah," Faith said.

"You need me, I'm in the next room," Celeste said. She was a good person to have Faith's back. She'd never had that feeling before Ryder.

"I'm okay."

A few seconds of silence passed after Celeste left the room. Ryder took a sip of his coffee and then set it down on the counter. His muscles were corded and his jaw clenched and released a few times before he spoke. "We need to talk."

"Before you say anything, Ryder. I owe you an apology," Faith said. She did. She owed him that and so much more. "I dragged you into this situation by blackmail. You're hurt and it's my fault. And worst of all, I didn't tell you the truth. I know you're angry and I don't blame you. All I can say is that I'll try to get better." She put her hand on her stomach. "I know what's at stake and I want to get along for the baby's sake. I also know that it's my fault we aren't. I should've told you everything about Michigan."

He stood there, looking momentarily stunned. And she could tell that he was contemplating what she'd said. She'd meant every word, and if he gave her a second chance she would do her best to include him in every way.

Ryder took in a sharp breath. "Everyone thinks my family is perfect. Well, I have a news flash. We're far from it. But we love and accept each other for who we are. We're honest with ourselves and each other. And that's good enough."

"I know," she said quietly.

"I can also see, especially after tonight, that you've never had anyone you could trust in your life before," he said, and her heart galloped with hope. "But we have to change if we want this to work. We have to learn to let each other in and talk about the future. I get that we've had a lot thrown at us in the past few days and we haven't exactly had time to process any of it and come up with a plan. But I need to know that you're not going to up and disappear on me. That we're doing this together. I think our child deserves that much from us, don't you?"

"I couldn't agree more," Faith said, wiping away a stray tear. She'd cried enough. She didn't want to cry again, hormones be damned. "I don't want us to end up anything like my family. Promise me that we won't let that happen."

"It's impossible. You're nothing like your family and I'm nothing like your father," Ryder said without hesitation, and that convinced her that he believed it. She would've hated if he'd believed that she was just another McCabe.

Their tentative agreement wasn't what Faith really wanted—she realized that she wanted Ryder—but this would be good for the baby and that was something to hold on to.

"You must think my family is crazy," she said. "I know I do."

"Lost maybe," he said, "not crazy. I don't think your mother or brother really thought this through. They could've killed us at any time tonight but they hesitated. Even your brother's shot was wide and he knows better."

"I blame my father for all of this. If he'd treated my mother like a human being none of this would be happening. He's a monster," she said simply.

"No. He's just a man. We all have darkness and light inside us. It's up to us to decide which one we chase."

Those words made her father seem beatable.

"When we found Nicholas, I'd planned to disappear," she said, figuring it was high time she came clean.

"And now?"

"I was afraid of my father. Still am. I'm scared of what he'll do when he finds out his daughter is carrying an O'Brien baby," she admitted, and it felt good to say those words out loud. She'd been holding so much inside for so long.

"I can see why you'd feel that way," Ryder said. "I'd never let any harm come to either one of you."

"He's sneaky. He manipulates. No one can guarantee my safety, Ryder. And, so, after I found out that I was pregnant, I got scared and stepped up my plans to disappear. I hated what I did to you, hated myself for lying and making you think that I'd walked away…that I'd gotten over you."

"You hadn't?" he asked.

"No, of course not. What we had was real to me. My father is powerful and he won't accept this. I'd hoped to disappear. Problem solved. Or, at least one problem was. I created another because I knew inside my heart that it wasn't fair to you or our child to keep you in the dark. I was too afraid to tell you what was really going on. You're a good person and you'd think that you could help."

"I could've and I can."

"I don't know. You can't watch over me 24/7. I have to go outside the ranch sometime. I didn't see a way out. And then Nicholas disappeared before I could execute my plan and I had nowhere else to turn."

"It's not a good feeling to be someone's last resort," he said.

"If I'm honest, I'd been stalling anyway. My home has been ready for weeks and I'd started stashing money in an offshore account a long time ago. Small amounts so my father wouldn't notice what I was doing. If he figured me out, it was over. I guess my mother was trying to do the same thing in her own twisted way. She was just doing it all in one shot. Now I have no idea what will happen to her."

"I'm surprised you care," he said.

"There's no way she should've missed at that close range," Faith said. She'd been brought up Texan, and that meant she knew her way around guns.

"I know." He held up his arm. "Your brother couldn't fake that bad of a shot. He tagged me anyway and I think it was meant to slow us down. He could've done a lot worse damage."

"The two of them working together? I never saw that coming," she said. "I guess they've both had enough. Jesse was always the most compassionate of my brothers. He'd been drinking more and more recently. I guess I've been too caught up in my own troubles to notice. And when I saw him earlier, I just saw desperation in both of their eyes."

"Like caged animals," Ryder agreed.

"I know I should probably hate both of them for what they did, but it makes me sad more than anything else that they've been pushed to this point. I know how desperate they feel because I've lived with it every day, too."

"And yet you didn't react in the same way," Ryder said.

"We're different people." She shrugged. "They made their choices. I just can't bring myself to hate them for trying to get away from my father. It blinded them to everything else and it made me realize that I have to face him. Going behind his back and hiding isn't me. He needs to know that I'm cutting him out of my life. I never want to see him again and he's no grandfather to my child."

"It's a risk I don't plan to take with you or the baby," Ryder said.

"You can come with me."

"I would. I'm just hoping that you'll listen when I say that you don't owe him anything. His emotions are going to be heightened when he realizes your mother and brother masterminded this whole plot against him, if he doesn't already know. I don't want you to leave the ranch for a while. I need you to be safe, and Dr. McConnell ordered bed rest," he said.

"Okay," she said after a thoughtful pause. "I don't have to deal with him right now if you're not comfortable with that. I'll face him once the baby's born. I need him to see that he can't break me." The look of relief on Ryder's face was worth giving in. She couldn't deny his points. Once Nicholas was found healthy and alive—because she wouldn't allow herself to think any other outcome was possible—she planned on focusing on having a healthy pregnancy.

"I have a question to ask…a favor," he started.

She nodded.

"Would you consider sticking around the ranch?" he asked. "At least until the baby's born, and then we can figure the rest out."

She didn't immediately respond. She hadn't given much thought to a plan B. Now that her entire life had changed she probably needed to learn to be more flexible. She also had some ground to make up with Ryder, and taking his ideas seriously would surely go a long way toward showing that she was ready to change, to let him in so he could begin to trust her. The threads were still very fragile. Plus, his suggestion had a nice ring to it. She'd be safe at the ranch and everything she needed would be provided. Maybe it was time to learn to go with the flow.

"Yes," she finally said, liking the smile that one word put on Ryder's face.

RYDER NEEDED TIME to figure out what he was going to do about his relationship with Faith. He saw a new maturity in her, and he was ready to take a few tentative steps toward working together for the sake of their child. Trust was still an issue but he could work toward finding a way to trust her again.

The past few hours without her had been pure hell. He told himself it was because he needed to know that she was okay for the sake of the baby. Anything more would just add to his confusing feelings for her. Confusing because Ryder didn't normally do second or third chances when it came to people he cared about. They let him down once and he'd always been more than willing to walk away. Faith was different. He wasn't ready to explore all the ways just yet. All he knew was that he felt more at ease when she was around and he knew she was okay.

"You should try to get some sleep," he said. "Everything that can be for Nicholas is being done tonight. Tommy said it's a good sign that the Hattie brothers saw him as innocent in all this and so wouldn't want to hurt him."

"My biggest fear is that he's out there, somewhere, alone. Scared. With no food or water," she said.

"We'll find him, Faith. Between us, my brothers, and two sheriff's offices, we'll bring him home safely."

Faith stood and started toward the guest room wing.

"Take my room," Ryder said. "McConnell was called in to check on a patient at the hospital and wants to stop by to check on my arm on her way home."

Besides, he had no plans to use his bed. He intended to stay up and go over the possibilities until he figured out where they'd keep Nicholas. In this process, Ryder had come to care for Celeste and couldn't turn his back on her any more than he could walk away from Faith.

Chapter Fourteen

Dr. McConnell had come and gone. She'd pressured Ryder into taking pain relievers for his arm that would also help him sleep. Faith crashed on the couch, her phone on her lap. The last thing he remembered was popping those two little pills in his mouth and then he'd gone down for the count.

So what was with feeling like he was being bounced around in a dryer?

Blinking his eyes open, Ryder tried to focus. Everything was a haze of yellow and orange, no doubt due to the pain meds. Concentrating was problematic.

There was a humming noise in his ears that he couldn't shake. McConnell must've given him strong medicine, because Ryder couldn't will his arms to move. What the hell? Was he even awake?

A burst of light passed over him and for a split second, he saw clearly.

Faith was across from him, eyes wide, tape secured over her mouth.

Ryder tried to speak, but couldn't. Then it dawned on him that he had tape over his mouth, too. He bit back a curse because he also realized that his hands were tied in front of him.

Somehow, and he had no idea how this could happen, there'd been a security breach at the ranch. Anger ripped through him that Faith was in danger once again.

They were traveling in some type of vehicle. Based on the size of the back area, an SUV. Thoughts of the Hattie brothers and Hannah crashed into Ryder's thoughts. A moment of sadness for the senseless loss of life pricked at him. It was replaced by determination.

Something was digging into his back. Hard. Metal.

Another burst of light revealed that someone was on the other side of Faith. His first thought was Celeste and that probably was right. If anyone managed to get inside the ranch and into his house, they'd had three people to deal with.

Ryder needed a plan. His ankles were bound together, so walking wasn't an option.

Where were they being taken? He had no idea how long they'd been in the SUV. Figuring out which road they were on was useless for now. As soon as the vehicle slowed, he'd try to pop up and get his bearings.

On second thought, the element of surprise was all he had going for him.

Ryder fought his instincts to blindly react to the situation.

Patience.

The SUV made a soft right. He'd heard the *click-clack* noise of blinkers so whoever was behind the wheel was being careful not to break any laws that could get him pulled over. Ryder was reasonably certain that the driver was male. It would take someone with superior strength to haul his dead weight into the SUV. Or the driver had help of some kind. Maybe someone who knew the ranch. He'd circle back with his brothers to discuss tightening security when he got through this ordeal. He refused to believe any other outcome besides survival was remotely possible.

Ryder listened for voices.

The SUV was quiet save for the purr of the engine, normally a sweet sound. This time, it felt like background music for attempted murder.

He kept the fact that he was awake from

Faith. One wrong move, her eyes diverting a second too soon, could give him away. He'd keep her as much in the dark as the driver hopefully was. Of course, he'd prefer that she wasn't involved at all. Since that option was outside his control, he'd work with what he had.

After a bumpy ride through what Ryder had to believe was woods, the SUV stopped. It was pitch-black outside, so they were obviously somewhere remote with no street lighting. The driver had veered off the main road at least fifteen minutes ago, which would be a safe enough distance to bury them alive if he wanted to without anyone noticing for weeks, months, possibly years.

The hatch slowly opened.

As soon as the bastard leaned in, he was going to get Ryder's heels in his face. If he could connect in the right place…

He shot his feet toward the blurry mass leaning toward him.

"Oh, no you don't," Hollister McCabe said as he caught Ryder's ankles.

McCabe? That thought didn't have nearly enough time to settle in as Ryder realized the man had a surprising amount of strength for being in his early sixties.

Faith tried to scream through the duct tape.

Ryder needed to communicate to her that she had to stay strong. He'd figure a way out of this mess. No way was Hollister McCabe going to be Ryder's downfall.

"Think you're going somewhere? Think again. Many people have tried to bring me down and failed," McCabe said, agitation clear in his voice. He would know by now that his wife and eldest son had betrayed him.

Ryder wished he could say, "Like your wife?" but the reminder might make McCabe even more determined to take his frustration out on Faith. Ryder couldn't afford to let that happen. McCabe's emotions would be even more raw now.

The next thing Ryder knew, he was being hauled out the back of the SUV. He dropped onto the ground with a thud and a grunt, having landed on his sore arm. He'd ducked so his head didn't slam into the bumper.

Feet hauled in the air, he flipped onto his back as he was being dragged into a wooden building of some sort, fighting against the pain shooting up his arm. A light flipped on and Ryder could see this place housed mowing and extra farm equipment.

Curled in a ball, bound and gagged, was another male frame. Even on his side, Ryder could see that the figure was tall and thin, the body of a boy who had yet to grow into his height. Nicholas.

McCabe mumbled unintelligible words as he tossed Ryder's feet toward the dusty wood floor and then disappeared. No doubt he was leaving to get Faith and the other person in the SUV Ryder believed to be Celeste.

He scooted toward the frightened teen.

Eyes wide, tearstained cheeks, there was no doubt this was Nicholas. The resemblance to Faith was evident.

Not being able to speak to calm the teen was frustrating. Ryder glanced around the room, looking for something—anything—he could use against McCabe. He tried to work the bindings on his arms with no luck. His legs netted the same result.

He had to slow down, to think. Joshua had told him how to break free from duct tape years ago when he was in some kind of law enforcement training. There was a way, if Ryder could remember. He hadn't been paying close attention, hadn't thought he'd ever need to know.

Another body was dragged in, kicking and fighting. Celeste.

A wave of panic shot through Ryder in thinking that McCabe would disappear with Faith. He forced steady breaths through his nose to keep his heart rate down. Fear would only feed the beast and cause him to make a mistake.

Ryder repeated his new mantra. *We're making it out of here alive.*

He thought back to his brother, to the duct tape.

The tape was easy to rip from an angle, he remembered, as McCabe disappeared again. He didn't close the door, and that was the first sign of hope that he was coming back.

Celeste was still kicking and screaming. Ryder needed to calm her down. Or maybe not...

Faith was dragged in next, and then positioned sitting up next to the door.

"You think you're going to betray me?" McCabe said. His voice had an eerie detachment to it as he ripped the tape off Faith's mouth.

"Say it," he demanded. "Tell them how you turned on me with that filthy mother and brother of yours. Did you really think you could use the Hattie family to outsmart me? I didn't want it to come to this, Faith. After all, you're my only girl. But you've turned on me."

"I have nothing to do with Mother and Jesse," she stated.

A menacing laugh tore from his throat. "You expect me to believe that? All three of you can burn in hell for all I'm concerned."

"Fine. Punish me. You won't believe that I'm not involved anyway. But the others here had nothing to do with it. None of this is their fault."

McCabe reached up high and then backhanded her across the cheek. Her head snapped left. She let out a cry that nearly broke Ryder's heart and renewed his resolve in the same beat.

"Everyone will pay for your betrayal." He sneered. "Just remember, all this is your fault."

"Please," she begged, "don't hurt them."

Ryder remembered what he needed to do. He needed to sit up in order to break out of the duct tape, remembering that his brother had said too often people freaked out and gave up when it didn't come off easily. Others fought it until they were too exhausted to keep going. Ryder had to admit that he'd fall into the second camp if he didn't know better. Many had died because they didn't know how easy it could be to rip. The method was specific, though. And Ryder needed space.

It would be impossible with Hollister McCabe in the room.

"I'm pregnant," Faith said, turning her face

toward her father. Shock had been replaced by anger.

Ryder didn't need her saying anything else to agitate her father, and those two words would surely do it.

"You think I don't know about the secret doctor's visits? Sneaking around behind my back? You put on a good show, though." His lip curled. "And now I know who the father is."

"How did you…wait, you had me followed. How long have you known?" she asked, so much anger in her voice. Which was another thing that could set McCabe off.

"For a while," he snapped.

Ryder was close enough to nudge Nicholas with his toe to get his attention. As it was, the boy lay on his side, crying.

Celeste tried to inch her way toward her boy. Ryder needed her to cause a scene in a different direction. He just needed a chance…

His opportunity came when McCabe stomped out of the shed, barn, whatever this building was. Using every ounce of energy he could muster, Ryder sat up. His abs burned but he managed it. He poked Nicholas's shin with his toe in order to get his attention. He had no idea how long he had before McCabe returned but he'd put money on not long enough.

With a bad arm, Ryder grunted as he put his arms over his head and pushed his elbows together. A forceful, downward motion and a quick burst out should rip the tape.

His first attempt netted zero unless he considered the intense pain.

"I don't hear him," Faith said quietly. "What can I do?"

Ryder shot her a look that said, "Stay put."

She took in a sharp breath and then scooted a little more toward the door.

Thankfully, with the explosion of pain came a burst of adrenaline. Celeste was still making her way toward Nicholas but he'd been focused on Ryder and was trying to break free of his bindings.

Ryder repositioned his arms, elbows together, hands above his head and gave it another try. Nothing. He was getting nowhere and McCabe could walk through that door at any second. With duct tape over his mouth he couldn't tell Faith to alert him the instant she heard footsteps. He assumed she would.

He squeezed his elbows together, hoping to create a tight seal. Hands high above his head and with a burst of energy, he pulled down and out. The rip echoed at the same time Faith warned that her father was coming.

Ryder glanced at Nicholas, who was still

struggling with the tape. Damn. It would've been useful to have his help. At least Ryder's arms were free even if the pain was blinding and blood covered his elbow and ran down his arm. He dropped to his side, as did Nicholas, and put his arms together in front of him so McCabe wouldn't realize what was going on.

McCabe stomped into the room and straight to the opposite corner, which had several cans of gasoline. Nicholas must've realized, too, because his crying amplified and Ryder had no way to calm him. He could only hope that he wouldn't anger McCabe further.

They had exactly three things going for them right now. One, Ryder's arms were free. Two, McCabe didn't know. Three, the old man was working alone.

How he got inside the ranch was a topic for another day. As for now, Ryder needed to make sure they'd be around to ask the question.

"You think I didn't know what you were up to, little girl," McCabe mumbled as he went about shaking the contents of the first gasoline container from the corner toward Ryder and the others in the middle of the room. "You're going to watch everyone you care about burn before you die."

"How did you find Nicholas?" she asked.

"The Hattie brothers sang like birds right before they died," he said and his voice had a hysterical quality to it.

Ryder pulled on all the strength he had to stay completely still, reminding himself of the stakes. Make a move too early and he'd give himself away. Give himself away and they had no chance of survival.

Unaware, McCabe moved closer, splashing the contents of the container on the floor in front of him as he walked. The contents were making a wide splatter as McCabe dragged his feet across the floor. He sprinkled some on Nicholas and Celeste. And then, Ryder. A few more steps.

Let him get close enough…

In one motion, Ryder swept McCabe's feet out from underneath him. The elder man came down hard with a grunt as he hit the wood floor.

Ryder's arm hurt like hell and the pain weakened him, but he couldn't allow himself to think about that right now. All he could focus on was bringing down McCabe. Grinding his teeth, Ryder pushed through the ache and used both arms to secure McCabe. The older man kicked and cursed, trying to wriggle out of Ryder's grip. The left arm was giving him trouble; the pain medication did little more than make him want to vomit and he was losing strength because of the blood loss.

On a normal day, McCabe would be no match for Ryder. Today was far from normal.

A boot slammed against Ryder's chin and his head snapped to the right. He caught a glimpse of Nicholas sitting up, trying to break his arms free. *Hurry.* Momentum was shifting in McCabe's direction and Ryder had no idea how much longer he could hold on.

Faith was shouting, and from the corner of his eye he could see that she was trying to break her hands free, as was Celeste. Any one of them succeeded and this fight would be over.

Gasoline was everywhere and had splattered them, which didn't help with the bile burning his throat, trying to force its way out. Ryder couldn't afford to let McCabe gain an inch. The older man's arms were free and Ryder had him by the thighs. He needed to hold on. Fists flew at him and then hands were grabbing at his face, poking at his eyes, pulling his hair. Ryder curled downward, angling his face away from McCabe. If they went up in flames, the old man was going with them.

McCabe was pulling out all the stops to try to break free. With Ryder's ankles still bound there'd be no way he could catch the old man if he broke out of Ryder's grasp. Worse yet, there was enough gasoline to light up the building with a single match. He could strike a match and lock the door behind him.

Ryder was losing strength. His arms felt like rubber. It was taking all his power, all his energy to hold on to the old man's legs. And then he heard the rip.

The hand gripped around his skull made it impossible to turn his head and look to see who was free.

A few seconds later, the hand was gone. Ryder looked up in time to see Nicholas on top of his father, holding his arms. Ryder held on to the man's thighs, making it impossible for him to kick, but he was trying to head-butt his son.

"What should I do?" Nicholas shouted.

Faith was scooting toward him, as was Celeste. There wasn't much either woman could do while they were tied up, and Ryder had exhausted all his strength getting this far. He wished he could tell Nicholas to grab something hard and bash his father in the head. That should slow McCabe down enough to set one of the women free.

He didn't have to. Faith did.

"I can't do it," Nicholas said, anguish in his voice.

In the big picture, it was probably for the best because it said a lot about the boy's character. However, in the moment it was problematic.

"He doesn't deserve to live," Faith said, managing to push up to her knees. "But if you can knock him out, we'll make sure he goes to jail for a very long time."

Faith was finally close enough to rip the duct tape off Ryder's mouth. His adrenaline was pumping too hard to feel the effects from the burn. Later, he'd pay for all of this.

"I can't hold on much longer," he said to Faith. "Put your hands up to my mouth."

She did.

He bit a small tear in her duct tape and she managed to free herself the rest of the way.

"You okay?" he asked with a glance toward her belly.

She nodded and then tore the tape from his ankles before freeing herself. She worked quickly and within thirty seconds had freed Celeste.

The scorned woman had no problem wielding the makeshift weapon. She stood over Hollister and said, "Your daughter and Ryder are going to make a beautiful family. You're an idiot not to see that Ryder will be more of a father than you'll ever be to any of your children. And I hope you enjoy your nap."

She winked at Nicholas and then swung the weed-whacker like a golf club. The casing cracked after making contact with the back of McCabe's skull, and he was immediately knocked unconscious.

He'd come around later behind cold, metal bars and have one hell of a headache to show for it, Ryder thought wryly.

They'd done it. Faith was safe. That was the only thought Ryder held on to as he gave in to the darkness pulling him under.

Chapter Fifteen

"Where's Faith?" Ryder broke through the fog long enough to ask. His body ached and he was being bounced around again. A sense of dread settled around him until he blinked his eyes open and realized he was in the back of an ambulance. There was an oxygen mask strapped over his mouth.

He lifted it and asked again.

"You're okay," the EMT said, obviously not understanding his question.

"Faith McCabe," Ryder said through searing pain, "where is she?"

"Ms. McCabe is fine. You, on the other hand, have lost a lot of blood." The man hunkered over Ryder was barely out of his twenties. "And I need you to put that back on."

He motioned toward the mask.

"I need to see her." Ryder tried to sit up

but was easily pushed back down by the strong EMT.

"You will," he said, and introduced himself as Carl. "She's in the car following us and we're almost there. As for now, I need you to let me do my job."

Ryder didn't have the strength to argue. He would take Carl on his word that Faith was okay, especially considering the fact that he was too weak to fight.

A few minutes later, the ambulance stopped and Ryder was being wheeled out the back strapped to a gurney.

"Hold up," Carl said to his partner and then winked at Ryder.

"Ryder," Faith shouted, as Carl waved her over.

Seeing her face gave Ryder new reason to fight the darkness tugging at him. He wanted to be fully awake so he could ask her the question that had popped into his mind the moment he considered the possibility that they both might die.

Nicholas was next to her and Celeste behind him as he took her by the hand.

"I'd get down on one knee if I could," Ryder started, suddenly unsure of himself in a way that he'd never experienced before. He'd push through the lack of confidence because she needed to know how he felt about her. "Because I don't want to live another minute without knowing you'll be there beside me every morning when I wake up. When I'm with you, I don't need to search for a thrill because just being with you makes me feel like I'm diving off a cliff, no safety net, in a way that I want to last forever. So I'm asking you to take me as your husband, your partner in this life. In turn, I promise to celebrate all the good times and be there to help you up every time you fall. Will you do me the honor of agreeing to marry me?"

Her moment of silence gripped him with fear that they'd never be able to get past their differences.

And then the wide smile broke across her face when she uttered the only word he needed to hear. *Yes.*

He tugged her down for a kiss before Carl broke it up and wheeled him into the ER and to the OR nurse waiting.

When Ryder woke the second time in a hospital room he was surrounded by everyone he loved. Faith sat on the edge of the bed. His brothers stood around, talking quietly. Nicholas and Celeste sat together in the chair by the bed.

He squeezed Faith's hand and she turned to him with a mix of worry and hope.

"Remember what you said earlier," he said with a wink. "Because I plan to hold you to it."

"Good. Because for a minute there I thought you were delirious before and wouldn't remember. I had no intention of letting you get away with it," she quipped. And her smile was all he needed to see. The rest of the people in the room were icing on a cake.

"Look who's finally awake," Joshua teased. And the others mumbled similar sentiments. They might be joking but Ryder knew just how worried they'd all been based on the lines creasing their foreheads and drawn around their mouths.

He thanked everyone for coming, and then reassured them that he was okay.

"Good. We didn't want to stand in line to see whose blood type matched up," Colin, one of his middle brothers, joked. Humor was the best stress reducer.

"You all should know that I've asked Faith to marry me," he said. "I love her and can't wait to be a family. I hope you'll be able to accept her in time, even if her last name is McCabe."

"Correction. Her last name is O'Brien,"

Dallas shot back. "And we wouldn't care what it was...she looks like she can keep you out of trouble and that's all that matters to us."

Congratulations broke out as each of his brothers hugged her one by one.

"You guys have never made me feel like an outsider," she said, wiping tears from her eyes. She glanced at Celeste and Nicholas. "And I hope you'll do the same for my family."

Dallas turned to Celeste. "Ryder filled us in on your situation and we'd like to offer you a job on the ranch. Janis is lonely in the big house and she's already preparing rooms for the both of you in hopes you'll accept."

"Wait. Hold on a minute," Ryder said to his brother. "How did you know I'd bring Faith home with me?"

"We're not stupid," Dallas said. "And neither are you, but you would've had to be to let her go."

"You guys really are going to make me cry like a baby," Faith said, turning to Ryder. "I've never felt so accepted or so much like home than when I'm with you."

"I don't want to be no charity case," Celeste said.

Nicholas started to protest, but she shushed him.

"I didn't say that I wasn't taking the job. I

just meant that I'll work harder than anyone else to prove I'm capable," she said.

"I have no doubt that you will," Ryder said.

Dallas agreed, kicking off another round of hugs and congratulations.

"Welcome to the family," Dallas said to Nicholas and Celeste. "One thing I've learned this year is that families only grow in love as they expand. I'm looking forward to growing ours with the two of you."

A nurse scurried into the room and then stopped when she saw the small crowd.

"I'm sorry to do this but I need everyone out," she said. Her name tag read Adeline.

"We'll be downstairs," Dallas said, leading the way out of the room.

"My future wife stays or I go with her, Adeline," Ryder said with a wink, pulling out all his charm. It must've worked because she fussed a little before agreeing.

Adeline checked his blood pressure and a few other things he didn't care about as he focused on the thought that he and Faith were going to be parents together.

A few minutes later, Adeline warned him about doing anything that would spike his blood pressure before she scurried out the door.

He laughed.

"We should probably check on your mother and Jesse," he said.

"Tommy called and said they were in trouble but since they hadn't intended for anyone to get hurt that the courts will most likely go light on them," she said. "He even said that he'd speak on their behalf if I wanted him to."

"And?"

"I do. My father will do everything in his power to make sure that she ends up with nothing, so I'm planning to offer my escape route to them once she serves her time." She looked at him and he could see warmth in her eyes. "I don't need it now that I have you."

"I meant every word of what I said before," he said to her. "I'm head over heels in love with you and I can't wait to make our family official."

"Want a shock?" she asked, and he couldn't read her expression.

Tears streamed down her cheeks when she rubbed her belly and said, "I think I've been in love with you from the very first day we met in second grade…and I can't wait to be Mrs. Ryder O'Brien."

Ryder pulled her down on the bed next to him and kissed the woman he loved, the mother of his child and his future wife.

* * * * *

Look for more books in USA TODAY *bestselling author Barb Han's miniseries* CATTLEMEN CRIME CLUB *in 2017.*

You'll find them wherever Harlequin Intrigue books are sold!